The Cabinet Maker

The Cabinet Maker

Nicole Johnston

ATHENA PRESS
LONDON

The Cabinet Maker
Copyright © Nicole Johnston 2006

All Rights Reserved

No part of this book may be reproduced in any form
by photocopying or by any electronic or mechanical means,
including information storage and retrieval systems,
without permission in writing from both the copyright
owner and the publisher of this book.

ISBN 1 84401 690 0

First Published 2006 by
ATHENA PRESS
Queen's House, 2 Holly Road
Twickenham TW1 4EG
United Kingdom

Printed for Athena Press

As a novel, this work is entirely a work of fiction. Though it contains incidental references to actual people, these references are used merely to lend the fiction an appropriate cultural and historical context. All other names, characters and incidents portrayed in this book are fictitious. Any resemblance to actual events or persons, living or dead, is entirely coincidental.

For Erin, Tara, Sofie, Neve, Cedar and Alyssa– may all your dreams come true!

Acknowledgements

Many thanks to my incomparable husband, Chris, who makes everything possible and to Mum for patiently putting up with my relentless requests for rereads. Thanks to my brother Gavin for exercising his creative genius in coming up with the title and to Mike for, yet again, proving to be a great mentor. And finally, my gratitude to Athena Press for helping me to bring a long-held dream to fruition.

Chapter One

His face buried in his considerable hands, fatigue washed over him as the realisation of his failure hit him once again. Everyone had finally left; the media that had been thronging for his attention only hours before had now evacuated in search of an interview with the man of the moment. Yet again he felt cheated of what was rightfully his. Oh God, he thought miserably, what do I do now?

He raised his head to survey the ruin that was once his office. Drink cans and bottles lay strewn across the surrounding desks and floor, drunk in commiseration rather than the celebration for which they had been intended. The staff had long since left, and his wife, though loath to leave him, had taken their children and his parents home. Rob for PM signs littered the floor – no longer needed. The bitter disappointment flooded over him once again. This had been his dream since childhood; his memory drifted back to the very first time he expressed what was later to become a passionate desire to lead his country.

He'd been nearly six, his long shorts, school tie and blazer inappropriate in the 38° heat of the Australian sun. His class had been asked to prepare presentations on what they wanted to do when they grew up. His presentation had followed a plethora of would-be teachers, lawyers and childcare assistants and something called a taxidermist. He felt strongly that his very good friend, Stephen, did not even know what one of those was – he had just been trying to impress the teacher. Now he was older, Rob thought wryly, he was sure that Stephen wouldn't have wanted to become a person who stuffed animals for a living. Rob had stood up at the front of the class and, with all the importance of a very small five-year-old, informed them that he wanted to be the Prime Minister. There had been a long pause followed by the very annoying, whiney voice of one of his classmates asking what a Prime Minister was. He remembered that moment, in particular, very clearly. He had informed them that the Prime Minister was the Boss of Australia. Yes, that was it – he had wanted to be the Boss of Australia.

Desolation struck again; he was never going to be the Boss of Australia now. His time was up; his moment in the sun was over. He had lost abysmally – yet again – to Peter Gooring, and had had to announce that he would be standing down as Leader of the Opposition to sit as a backbencher. His sense of loss was palpable as he let go of his lifelong dream to lead his country. At this precise moment it felt unbearable, the weight of it making it hard to breathe.

He heaved his fatigued body out of his chair, his crumpled suit showing signs of what had been an extremely long day. The TV silently showed the triumphant PM walking amongst his supporters, gloating in that smug way that only Gooring could. He suddenly felt angry. He had won the primary votes and the preferences, so he should be Prime Minister now. What had gone wrong? Labor had won its extra votes in the seats it had already held – that's what had gone wrong. It was a rare event: the PM had won the election with 36% of the vote, including preferences. In a country with compulsory voting that was pretty ordinary, even for Gooring. But Gooring would bumble along, pretending a God-given right to govern, as he had done for the past nine years.

The anger left him almost as quickly as it had come, replaced again by the torturous disappointment, which was to stay with him for many months. He ambled out of the door, taking care to lock it as he left. A lone figure sat in a car in the car park and Rob wandered over to get in beside him. The man in the driver's seat turned to him with one eyebrow raised in question. Rob's answering gaze ensured no further discussion, and John, his driver, simply backed out of his parking bay and took the new backbencher home.

John felt inordinately sad for the man sitting beside him. As a Government driver he was supposed to be impartial, but he had come to like Rob. Rob's quiet intelligence and genuine desire to change things for those less well off than himself had impressed him. Not that he always agreed with his policies – no way! There were a few times that John had had to bite back comments when he had heard those advising Rob on how he should stand on certain issues. But he grew to understand that despite this Rob's decisions came from a good place. Take now for instance: every other politician he had driven sat in the back seat treating John like a chauffeur, but Rob sat in the front with him. He knew all of John's children's names, that his wife had MS, and exactly what the doctors were treating her with at any given time. He had even taken time to visit Abby in the hospital.

They made the drive home in silence, watching the city reveal itself slowly to them as they made their way down the freeway. The city lights were at their brilliant best seemingly unaware of the election result. John stopped outside Rob's pretty weatherboard cottage and turned to him, saying quietly, 'I really am sorry, Rob, I really thought it was yours this time.'

'I know… Thanks for that, mate, I really did too,' replied Rob moving away from the car.

John left Rob standing despondently at his front door, appearing unwilling to go inside immediately.

Chapter Two

Robert Joseph Connor was born on 1 June 1954 to a public servant and a school librarian. Both were doting parents of their only progeny, and were forever assuring him that he could achieve anything. Under their admiring gaze he had done well at school, particularly at high school. He was a capable sportsman, particularly at cricket. This did not, however, include football, at which he genuinely appeared to have two left feet.

His schooldays were largely happy, marred only by the loss of his favourite grandmother, Mavis. She had died of complications following a stroke when he was twelve and he had missed her terribly for many years. 'Nanna Parky', as she had been known because her last name was Parkinson, was his mum's mother. She had a wicked sense of humour, often seeing the funny side of Rob's naughtier escapades, where his mother could not. Nanna Parky had always smelt so nice, lathered in talc and Tweed perfume. She was, he had always thought, a 'real' Nanna, someone who other young children had approached in shopping centres. Even now he felt her loss keenly.

Always willing to express his opinion whenever the opportunity presented itself, high school debating saw him begin to develop the skills of presenting his argument that were to assist him greatly in his later years.

Debating required him not only to research his argument and ensure that it was robust but to present it eloquently and convincingly.

High school was an easy time for him; he had prioritised his studies at an early age, feeling sure that he would have to go to university if he was to stand any chance to become the leader of his country. The risk of him being isolated because of his commitment to study was lessened by the fact that he was an equally committed cricketer. His patience and skill was reflected in both of his primary pursuits.

At an early age he became aware of the distinct difference between those who had money and opportunities and those who did not. His own family made ends meet reasonably comfortably, but many of the families of his close school friends did not. In his early teenage years one of his school friends had a father who worked on the mines and was sacked after he was injured on-site. He was then forced out of his home with his family after the bank foreclosed their mortgage. This situation made a huge impact on Rob's young life, as he found it difficult to understand why James' father's employer was not required to pay some sort of compensation, given that their former employee was not ever able to work again. Rob felt sure that the mining company was responsible for the dreadful situation that had very negatively affected his friend and his friend's family.

He discussed this situation at length with his parents and they agreed strongly with his view. His father suggested that he consider the role of the unions.

Rob left high school with sound marks and made his way to university. He started university as Gough Whitlam came into power and the country had been swept with an overwhelming sense of optimism. It was at this point that he became aware of his political affiliation. How could he be anything but Labor? He had reached this conclusion as he watched 'the Big Man' push reforms through in many areas that had previously been ignored. It was amazing, he thought with awe, what one man and his Government could do in a few short years, after that Menzies fella had done virtually nothing in nearly a quarter of a century, through one of Australia's greatest boom times.

In this breathtaking era Rob's hair got longer, his clothes got brighter and he developed a long-standing love affair with appalling neckwear. It was a love affair his mother tried valiantly to counter, making a regular gift of ties that sadly found their way into the Salvation Army clothes bins at the earliest opportunity.

He watched as Whitlam reshaped Australia, breathless with anticipation. His father, a traditional Labor supporter, was less glowing in his assessment of the new Government's attempts. While extremely pleased 'in principle' with the objectives of this Government, his innately small 'c' conservative nature balked at the rapid pace of change and the perception of a lack of transparency.

University was a playground for the young Rob. He discovered like-minded people and met with politically informed men and women who were to influence his opinions for many years to come. He joined the local university branch of the Labor Party and threw himself into its work with gusto. Finding himself an office holder within a very short time, he soon impressed others with his keen intelligence and his commitment to developing his knowledge and opinions. He had, during this time, the opportunity to meet many leading lights in his Party.

Then it happened, an event that was to mark his cards for the rest of his career: the Governor-General, the unelected representative of the Queen in Australia, sacked Whitlam. 11 November 1975 was to bring Australia as close to civil war as it had ever been.

Just as a resolution to an impending crisis that could have led to the Government having no money was determined, John Kerr forestalled its resolution and threw the PM out in favour of Opposition Leader, Malcolm Fraser.

As was true of most in Australia at that time, Rob remembered for the rest of his life where he was when he heard the news. In a rare attempt to meet all of his lecture commitments, possibly influenced by impending end of year exams, Rob was sitting at the uni café drinking very bad coffee and revising Property Law. He vaguely heard, as if in the distance, the café owner shouting over the noise of the throng of students telling them to shut up. He turned the radio up as far as it would go and the devastating news burst forth.

'Gough Whitlam has been sacked, sacked, sacked,' the ABC newsreader stated in an overly melodramatic fashion.

Rob felt as though someone had punched him very hard in the stomach. He could not breath and he felt like he needed to throw up. The usually noisy café was strangely silent and then a young woman broke the silence with a loud sob that sounded remarkably like a loud '*No!*' Suddenly the room was filled with shocked voices and people crying.

Rob left his revision on the small table and sprinted to the Labor Party's branch office on campus. The red eyes and shocked stares told him that they had already heard the news. The tiny portable radio was on one of the two small desks in the office and a crowd had formed around it. Disbelief, grief and anger were evident in different stages in the room. Rob was overcome with an overwhelming sense of denial even as Gough started to speak.

'Well, may we say "God save the Queen"; because nothing will save the Governor-General,' he boomed through the ludicrously inadequate transistor.

Rob was floored, the impossible was true: Whitlam had actually been sacked. He slid to the floor with a thump. Around him fresh tears were brewing. He buried his face in his hands, wishing that he could simply wake up from what had become one of his worst nightmares.

As is to be expected amongst students the grief quickly turned to the need for action. They proposed protests, petitions and not much short of civil revolt.

'It can't be legal, no it can't be legal!' exploded the Branch Secretary. They all hastily agreed, but then no one knew quite what it was they could do about it.

They were startled during their frantic plans to hear the voice of Bob Hawke, the darling of the union movement, on their small radio begging for calm. He stated that it was important to maintain the rage but not to respond with violence.

They were instantly deflated. What to do now? One by one the grief-stricken students wandered away unsure of what to do or where to go.

Rob wandered back to the café in search of his abandoned books and notes. Miraculously, they were exactly where he had left them. The café was filled with an eerie silence, students looking more than a little shell-shocked. He gathered up his books and decided to head home, sure that he couldn't concentrate on his lectures anymore that day. All around him the campus was filled with little huddles of people looking desolate. Even those he recognised as having Liberal leanings were looking stunned.

He arrived home to find both his mother and father sitting as though waiting for him at the kitchen table, absently drinking coffee. He never did ask them how it was that they were both at home at 11 o'clock on a workday. He reached his father first who, while not normally a man comfortable with showing emotion, held fast to his son while Rob finally let go of the shock, disappointment and grief that had not yet had an opportunity to be expelled.

His mother furnished him with a hot, sweet cup of coffee. They all sat down around the kitchen table in silence for some time.

The next morning Rob rose early. When they were all sitting around the kitchen table again he announced to his parents that if it took him the rest of his life he would make sure Australia became a republic and ensure that never again could an unelected representative of a foreign power dismiss an elected representative of the Australian people. And in that moment a policy was born.

The rest of Rob's university career went reasonably smoothly in a flurry of papers, exams, Labor Party meetings and functions. He surprised himself by being offered a scholarship to complete a Master of Laws degree after finishing his first degree with a high point average.

Rob left university, and rather than finding himself completing his Articles, as most of his colleagues chose to do, he went to work for the Miscellaneous Workers' Union as an organiser. This period fuelled Rob's passion for fairness, equality and justice. He became a zealot on the issues of racism and discrimination anywhere, but particularly in the workplace. The next few years disappeared in a blur of meetings, protests and Party functions. They were heady years, and by the time he turned twenty-five Rob had met all of the movers and shakers in WA politics – including Bob Hawke, who had taken a shine to the young, clever and articulate Rob. Bob Hawke was himself a West Australian and was touted to become a future Prime Minister. Rob was impressed by this man's charisma and ability to communicate with ordinary people.

When Bob Hawke was elected to Parliament in October 1980, Rob was heavily involved in the election campaign. It was an exhilarating experience, the hours were unbelievable and Rob spent most of his spare time dealing with mounting exhaustion. Those working on the federal election campaign worked hard and played hard. That the stakes were so high – to run Government or to spend another three years in Opposition – added to the adrenaline they all felt. There was camaraderie between the young people working on the campaign, despite a very strong sense of competition. Many of them were positioning themselves in the event that Labor took the election. Undoubtedly, there would be many jobs for those who had worked on the campaign.

The feeling Rob had was that he was exactly where he was meant to be at that precise time in his life. His sense of fate was overwhelming now and he knew that he was on the edge of something really important. He felt strongly that he had part in influencing history.

Late in 1980 Rob was offered a job as an Electorate Officer for one of the new Federal Members of Parliament. His new MP, John Wilcox, was a big man with a big heart and a fantastic sense of humour. Far from being overwhelmed by this new task he seemed to live in a permanent state of surprise. His white beard and ruddy face made him look like Father Christmas, and Rob was sure that this was part of the reason that the people in his electorate warmed to him so much. People who came to see 'Johnno', as he was more commonly known, for help with their tax, social security, education and employment issues were always in a much happier mood by the time they left, no matter how irate they'd been on arrival. His booming laugh could be heard all over the office and it always made Rob smile. He often used to wonder what could possibly be amusing about a situation in which people were being wrongly accused of defrauding social security, and all because of a mistake by the Department of Social Security itself!

After a few short months, Johnno began to allow Rob to sit in on the appointments and watch him in action. Rob was amazed by the MP's capacity to relate to the many and varied people who asked him for help. Wherever he was able to help, Johnno would act immediately. He would use the appointment time to phone the department concerned or type up a letter on his constituent's behalf. Rob knew from his fellow Electorate Officers that this was unusual. Many sat on requests for weeks or even months before acting. Before long Johnno was allowing Rob to take on cases himself, and this virtually doubled the number of matters the office was able to deal with.

Rob would never forget the day that it was his turn to accompany Johnno to Canberra. He was enamoured with the country's capital on his first visit. Although it was a very small city it was perfectly laid out, with Lake Burley Griffin in the foreground shining in the sun. The day was cold and the wind of the mountains took his breath away, cutting through his jacket as though it was as flimsy as silk. It rarely snowed in Canberra, but Mother Nature turned on its very best for him and the city looked like it was coated in icing sugar.

But it was Parliament House that really did it for him. The grand old building on the banks of the lake filled him with a sense of being where the action was. He walked through the narrow halls with nothing short of veneration, loving its musty smell; in some strange way it reminded him of his Nan's place in Mount Lawley. The legend was that most of the deals done in Parliament were actually agreed in these corridors of power. Whitlam had walked these floors and, if the truth were known, he still did on occasion, offering his wisdom and opinions to the Opposition when they did (and did not) want them.

Two great events were to happen here in very short order, and they would change his life for ever.

One day, racing through these hallowed halls, he collided with the most amazing looking woman he had ever seen. At twenty-four, Maggie Turnbull had a shiny mane of hair and the most startling blue eyes. Rob was less than eloquent in his apologies for knocking the pile of briefings out of her hand. In fact, he positively stuttered, momentarily forgetting where it was he was supposed to be going.

Maggie smiled disarmingly, displaying perfect teeth and one loppy dimple. She then proceeded to lecture him harshly on running through the narrow halls. But by then Rob was totally, utterly in love.

Maggie, however, was not. Having retrieved her briefings, she went on her way. Not being quite himself, Rob didn't even think to ask her name or where she worked before she disappeared into the rabbit warren of offices that made up Parliament House.

Within hours Rob, uncharacteristically ignoring the ever increasing pile of work on his desk, had identified the mystery woman and where she worked. He was more than a little dismayed to discover that she worked for a Liberal Minister as a Research Officer. He was positively grief stricken to discover further that she was the only daughter of a Liberal Senator, Senator Geoffrey Turnbull. He spent the next few weeks unsuccessfully trying to forget those unforgettable blue eyes...

The second event came in his next visit to Parliament House with Johnno. He was a touch jet-lagged after catching a red-eye the previous evening, having a shower and coming directly into work. At 10.30 Bob Hawke arrived. Rob, expecting that he had an appointment with Johnno, organised a cup of coffee for Bob and advised him that Johnno would be in directly. Bob asked him if there was a quiet place that they could have a chat. Rob was surprised, but organised a small office off the kitchen and cleared some papers off the tiny desk. Bob sat down and, being the direct sort of person that he was, launched into the startling reason that he had come to see him. He asked if Rob knew that Malcolm Bent, MP for Wilson in Western Australia, had died unexpectedly the previous day. Rob nodded that he had been made aware of this tragic event. Bob advised that a federal election was due at any time and that, as Mal had been a sitting MP, there had not been a particularly robust pre-selection process. As a result they had no one available to replace him. Rob nodded a second time, wondering how this could possibly involve him; but given the massive amount of respect he held for the man sitting in front of him he was unwilling to interrupt his flow.

Bob simply looked Rob straight in the eye and said, 'Well, son, are you up for it?'

At first Rob was unclear as to what Bob was proposing. Surely, he thought, there were people better qualified than him to find a replacement for Mal! He looked enquiringly at Bob, only to be answered with an amused grin. Then a seed of something started to grow in his addled brain. There was surely no way that Bob was suggesting that he run as the Labor Candidate in Wilson was he? A further look at Hawke's face revealed that this was exactly what he was proposing.

Within weeks, in a blur of activity, Rob Connor had been confirmed by both the Wilson Electorate Committee and the State Executive as the Labor Candidate in Wilson. Rob was stunned; he had been involved with the Labor Party long enough to know that this was not the manner in which pre-selections were usually conducted. However, in this case there was little option. Within months Bob Hawke had been confirmed as Leader of the Opposition in place of Bill Hayden and the Government had announced a federal election. Rob felt dizzy at the pace with which his life had changed.

His parents' mood was mixed. They were terrified that their son was in over his head and immensely proud of him at the same time. Johnno was beside himself that his entirely competent Electorate Officer was set to be one of his colleagues in Parliament.

The lead up to the election was exhausting, with endless interviews with journalists, letter box drops and door-knocking. Rob's hand nearly lost the will to live with the number of letters he was required to sign. On the day before the election, when he felt that he could not walk one more step or sign one more letter, he was buoyed by a phone call from his erstwhile leader wishing him luck. The adrenaline kicked in with a vengeance, and he was soon out on the trail again, trawling shopping centres, stopping to hear the concerns of voters as he went.

Election day began at 5 a.m. Rob felt that he could not be asleep while his polling booth workers would be up setting out posters and pamphlets in advance of the early morning rush of voters who needed to get to work. Not that it mattered; he certainly hadn't been able to sleep anyway. He found himself sitting on the verandah of the lovely weatherboard cottage he had bought in the Wilson electorate, feeling strongly that a person could not properly propose to represent an electorate without living and working there. He had been very concerned about purchasing his first home in such a hurry, but had managed to scrape together a deposit, and had felt a mix of relief and elation when he had first seen this cottage in Pemberton Street. He had known immediately that however long he had had to look for his first home this would always have been his choice. It was cream and white outside with wooden floorboards and high ceilings with original cornices.

The verandah he sat on spanned the front of the small cottage and had white roses growing wild over the lattice. He could smell their sweet fragrance even from where he was sitting at the small iron table his mother had found for him in a second-hand store. He smiled as he saw the neighbour's two brown speckled ducks walking companionably up the street. It was impossibly twee, but he really felt at home in this strange little street.

He had just finished his first coffee when the phone rang, and he sighed, realising that it signalled the last peaceful moment for that day. The call was from his Campaign Manager and he jumped into his old VW Beetle and headed for the office.

The day progressed well with only several hundred crises that needed to be dealt with immediately. Pamphlets and 'how to vote' cards ran out, and more drinks and sandwiches needed to be organised because of the enormous number of volunteers who had come out to work on the polling booths. However, nothing could mar the sense of optimism that prevailed.

The polling booths closed at 6 p.m., and the candidate and his team retired back to his campaign office.

The team of volunteers made themselves comfortable all over the conference room where a large television was perched on the table to watch the incoming results. Rob followed his Campaign Manager, Astrid Barber, through to the more quiet inner offices, where a smaller TV was set up, with a whiteboard to record the incoming results from the polls. Now that the frantic activity had ceased Rob found it impossible to sit still. He paced the floor endlessly until Astrid, laughingly, reminded him that it was going to be a long night as the results weren't due for hours. Finally he sat down, restlessly watching as Tom Bennett, the local stats expert, tallied up the results from the local polling booths as they came in.

Rob popped in regularly to check on the volunteers, the people who had got him through the election in one piece, to see how they were going. The group was buoyed by the incoming results from the rest of the country. Given the time difference, the Eastern states were significantly ahead in their polling results. However, Rob suspected that they were also somewhat buoyed by the amount of beer and wine they had managed to put away since their arrival, the evidence of which was littered all over the room.

He took himself outside for a quiet moment and his mind wandered reluctantly to Maggie Turnbull. He knew at this very moment she would be with her father, the heavy-hitting WA Liberal Senator. He had been elated to discover that she was from WA. The chances of that had been pretty slim he had to concede, but this was heavily outweighed by the fact that she was a Liberal. It was impossible, he knew that for sure. Even if she had been able to go out with someone so significantly involved in politics for the opposite side, he certainly couldn't. However, they had wound up flying back to WA on the same flight some months ago and he was overwhelmed by how attracted he was to her. She was simply the most beautiful woman he had ever seen. She was wearing a smart navy suit and had greeted him with a very sharp nod and then proceeded on her way. Inexplicably, this had only attracted him more. He had to be realistic, though; even if they could get past the political differences, she was clearly not the slightest bit interested in him. He shook his head as if to clear it of the thoughts that had distracted him from the matter at hand.

Back in the office the numbers were looking very good – no doubt due to Mal Bent's considerable personal support and the sympathy vote, Rob thought grimly. A shout came from the volunteers' room. Rob and his team turned their attention to the small TV, and were startled to see that the commentator had said that if Labor won two more seats Hawke would claim victory. Rob was stunned. Only half his polling booths had reported in and yet the election was nearly decided. Momentarily he panicked. What if the election was won and he lost his seat? Then he reminded himself that that was not the issue. For the good of the country it was important that Labor won Government; it was not important whether he won his seat or not.

Now refocused on what mattered, he turned his attention to the television. A jubilant Hawke was taking his place at the podium declaring victory. A shout went up from all over the small office, and Rob heard himself cheering loudly, filled with elation at the return of a Labor Government.

He turned to see Tom Bennett smiling at him in his quiet, calm way. Tom said, 'It seems you are off to Canberra too, Rob.'

Rob smiled and nodded and turned back to view the elated celebration on the television. Suddenly he spun back to face the quiet man, his eyes open wide.

Tom laughed and said, 'Yep, it's official – you are the Federal Member for Wilson.'

Rob stopped and stared, scarcely able to believe what he had just heard; and then with a shout, began jumping up and down on the spot, arms flailing. The immensity of what he'd achieved caught up with the whole room. His colleagues, all aware by now that he was on his way to Canberra, laughed, cheered and cried in equal measure.

He walked through to the office kitchen where his parents were sipping cold coffee. They had retreated there some hours earlier when they were unsure quite how to relate to this very strange crowd of tired and exuberant people. He looked at their expectant faces and gave them a huge grin.

His mother looked at him and asked hesitantly, 'Do you mean Labor won the election – or you have won your seat?'

They both stood staring intently at him awaiting for his response.

'All of the above!' he shouted.

His father and mother grabbed him and the three of them danced jubilantly around the small kitchen. Truth be told he knew that his parents didn't really understand why this was so important to him or how this political bug had managed to get under his skin. However, they were both very proud of him, and very excited that he had achieved so much at such a young age.

Later Rob watched footage of Malcolm Fraser with his eyes filling with tears as he conceded defeat. But Rob felt no sympathy for the man who had replaced Gough Whitlam in 1975. In Rob's opinion he'd had no right to be there in the first place.

Six weeks later, the new Member for Wilson joined his colleagues on the Government benches in the House of Representatives. He was delighted with his poky new office and had managed to employ two full-time electorate officers. He was amazed that Mal's Senior Electorate Officer had agreed to stay on with him – Eleanor, the wife of the quiet but efficient statistician from election night, was a godsend. Within two short weeks she had him organised and house-trained in his new Electorate Office.

The second Electorate Officer was a young man, a teacher, who was a much bigger risk. He had limited experience, but Rob hoped that Reg's teaching experience would assist him to deal patiently and compassionately with constituent enquiries. He would have to employ a further staff member to deal with reception and his diary, but he had not yet had time to do this and felt sure that Eleanor was on the case anyway.

As the months progressed Rob quickly learnt the disadvantage of being an MP. The flights on Sunday nights to get to Canberra always had to go through one of the other major cities and ended up taking the best part of seven hours – and that didn't count the waiting in airports for connecting flights. He would arrive at the flat he shared with two other MPs just before 11 p.m., make himself a quick cuppa and go to bed, his hands full of letters he had to sign and papers to read before reaching his office the next day. He thought that he'd had some idea of the amount of work he was in for because of his time with Johnno, but he had clearly had no clue.

He would sleep until 6.30 a.m., shower quickly, dress and then dive into a pre-ordered taxi to get to Parliament House. His days were filled with constant letters, papers, meetings – and, of course, Parliament.

Then on Thursday evening it would be back on a plane and home to Perth, again via another capital city. He had thought more than once, that there could not be another capital city in the Western world that did not have direct flights to it.

On his return he would usually arrive at about 11 p.m. Perth time, 1 a.m. in Canberra, and get home to his cottage by 11.30 p.m. The routine was the same as Canberra, except that when he closed the door to his cottage on Pemberton Street he felt truly relaxed and at home. He would put a wash in the machine, treat himself to a glass of wine and then throw himself into bed with glee. At 7.30 a.m. he would be up to hang the washing, collect his dry-cleaning and head off to the office for a day of constituents and community groups. Weekends, more often than not, required him to attend party functions or events in his constituency, where he would be required to speak. However, he always found time to call or visit his parents on Sunday, trying to get to their place for Sunday lunch if at all possible.

On Sunday evening the process would start again, and by the end of the year he was exhausted and desperate for the Parliament to rise for Christmas.

Soon, despite the tiring pace, Rob fell into some sort of routine, and time flew by. He found there was some advantage to the many flights between Perth and Canberra, as he saw a great deal of Maggie. On one occasion he and Maggie were seated together on a plane that was delayed for an hour and a half at Perth Airport for reasons known only to an obscure air traffic controller. As the air stewards frantically delivered coffee, tea and water to their passengers and apologised for the unexpected delay, Maggie and Rob were forced to speak through pure politeness.

Rob finally mustered the courage to ask how she was and Maggie answered with a characteristically curt, 'Fine.' For some reason that was unclear, this amused him and inspired him to try harder to get her to break her long-running, self-imposed silence and have a full conversation.

An hour later, Rob was regretting his lack of caution in relation to this lovely young lady. She was tearing strips off him in front of their fellow passengers, who were thoroughly enjoying the loud distraction from the lack of activity on their chosen mode of transport. He vaguely heard the words 'tree-hugging liberal' and had decided that she was the biggest bitch he had ever met and, much more importantly than that, he was deeply and terminally in love... He smiled at her despite himself and she looked at him, momentarily losing her flow. But momentary it was, and she was back at it, the words 'high tax, high spend' assaulting his ears. But it was not until she made the mistake of accusing the PM of being a 'lightweight' that he felt he'd had enough. The other passengers watched in rapt silence as he deftly obliterated her argument on the PM's 'lightweightedness', advised her (with appropriate evidence) that Australia was one of the lowest taxed countries in the OECD, and his Government did have a commitment to schools, hospitals, universities and roads that worked, and it all required investment. Finally he told her that if 'tree-hugging liberal' meant that he cared about the low income and disadvantaged people of his country then, yes, he would be proud to wear that label. Running out of breath, he stopped long enough to see her grinning at him.

'Not bad for a socialist!' she remarked, amused and,

it seemed, perhaps just a little impressed.

After several hours of quieter discussion on the pros and cons of conservatism versus socially democratic values, they were both surprised to discover that the plane had landed in Melbourne, and they needed to transfer to their Canberra-bound flight. Unfortunately they were not on the same connecting flight. Rob said goodbye and added that he would very much like to continue the discussion at a later date. To his amazement Maggie agreed. He watched her as she walked away, feeling more than a little disappointed that the flight had not been longer. He laughed at the irony of that thought, given how many times he had quietly cursed the length of these flights. On this occasion he would happily have flown around the world twice just to have extended their conversation. Sighing, he turned and made his way across the airport to his connecting flight.

Two days later he was surprised to see a phone message from Maggie in the unenviable pile of paper on his desk. He immediately began dialling her extension number and then got cold feet. Hesitating for some minutes before raising the earpiece again, his heart pounding furiously, he pressed the numbers once more. Maggie sounded very pleased to hear from him and asked whether he had time for a quick cup of coffee later that morning. Not surprisingly, Rob found time to fit her into his busy schedule.

The coffee in the cafeteria was terrible, but the company was great. Rob was amazed at how easy she was to speak to – when they weren't fighting. Maggie was intelligent, articulate and prepared to fight her corner. It had been a long time since a woman he was attracted to had challenged him in a debate on policy. She'd made him rethink about how robust his views really were, although he kept that to himself. He had felt compelled to ensure that his views were well evidenced and nothing less than watertight, if only to stop her wiping the floor with him in their debates.

As the weeks and months wore on, the two met more and more often, over coffee, lunch and even dinner. Rob found it hard not to think of her when he was trying to work. He knew that she was the only girl for him, but he really couldn't work out how to get around the fact that they were from opposite sides of the political spectrum. Although, in practice they agreed on many of their principles, their ideal methodologies differed significantly. As well as this she worked for a Liberal MP, and her father was a powerful Liberal senator. He agonised about this endlessly, unprepared to believe that where there was a will there wasn't a way, but was unable to work out a solution. Especially now that he was an MP; he could hardly just quit, could he? What could he do?

Little did he know that the problem was to resolve itself. One Friday night at about 10 p.m. he was having a rare quiet moment sitting on his front verandah drinking a glass of Merlot and reading the latest John Grisham novel when a small white sedan pulled up beside his VW Beetle. He looked up, curious to see who his visitor was, squinting against the street light. He was stunned to see Maggie walking tentatively up the three steps to the verandah, clearly agitated. Rob walked towards her, feeling very concerned all of a sudden about her unexpected appearance at such a late hour.

'Maggie, are you okay?' he asked, dread filling his stomach.

'Yeah – I think so... Well, that depends,' she answered cryptically.

Rob, even more confused, asked her to sit down and went to retrieve another wine glass for her.

When he returned she was standing up again, looking out at the street.

'Do you... oh God I feel so stupid!' she said, as she paced up and down the small verandah. Then, taking a deep breath as if steeling herself, she said, 'Do you love me, Rob?'

Rob was momentarily stunned, then seeing the anguish creep back over her face, he hurriedly replied, 'Of course – of course I love you! But I just don't see how it can work with your father...'

She laughed. 'That's it – that's what is stopping you saying anything... doing anything? My father?'

Rob was very confused 'He is a Liberal Senator, I am a Labor MP. This is not exactly a match made in heaven.'

Maggie's face changed, a storm brewing 'You're not marrying *him* – you're marrying *me!*' she exploded.

'*Marrying* you... getting married? Oh my God, are you saying that you want to marry me?' Exclaimed

Rob. But he didn't wait for an answer, he swept forward and took her in his arms, his mouth reaching for hers. Later he wondered whether he had just done this so that he didn't have to hear a negative answer.

As they finally got to their glasses of wine, he asked Maggie what her parents really thought of her marrying him. Maggie replied with a cheeky grin that they had realised some time ago that she was smitten, and had resigned themselves to the fact that marrying her off to a nice little conservative boy was simply not going to happen! She laughed as she recounted a conversation where her father had indicated that her choice of husband was consistent with her lifelong unconventional and often rebellious approach to life.

Rob asked how she felt about marrying a Labor MP when she was so clearly a Conservative. Maggie's reply warmed his heart. She said that while she wasn't a supporter of the Labor Party she was supportive of him personally, adding with a mischievous grin, 'And my vote is my choice and confidential.'

Rob laughed, a touch shell-shocked that he was going to get to marry the woman of his dreams. They talked long into the night, something he knew he would seriously regret the next day at his early Electorate Council meeting. Those meetings were often interminably dull and laborious, without adding the disadvantage of having had no sleep.

However, the next day he woke with a spring in his step. The sun was shining and the birds were singing. The neighbour's ducks were happily waddling down

Pemberton Street. His meeting went well, and afterwards he rang Maggie, ostensibly to say 'Hi' but really to ensure that the whole encounter had not just been a glorious dream. She was in bed still – not that he was surprised by that, given the time she would have finally arrived home. He was gratified and not a little relieved to note that the woman who answered the phone was very friendly, and assured him that she would let Maggie know that he had called as soon as she woke up.

A very short time later his phone rang and he answered, hearing a very cheery voice on the other end. He paused a moment before being brave enough to ask whether Maggie would consider coming to lunch with him and his parents the following day. She replied immediately that she would love to, but he heard a touch of nervousness in her voice – a rare emotion for her, he suspected.

The next day he picked Maggie up twenty minutes early, aware that it would be a good idea to take the opportunity to meet her parents, his future in-laws, before sweeping her off to lunch with his mum and dad. It wasn't until he knocked on the front door of the grand old Mount Lawley property that his nerves started to really affect him. He was in the process of taking several deep breaths to get a hold of himself, when the door opened to reveal an elegant, older version of his Maggie.

There was a bright and welcoming smile on his hostess's face as she introduced herself as Ingrid,

Maggie's mother. She took Rob through to Maggie's father, Geoff, who surprised Rob immensely by being an outgoing man who was very easy to feel comfortable with. Despite their political differences, which they kept to themselves, it appeared that Geoff and Ingrid were content with Maggie's decision. They certainly pulled out all of the stops to ensure Rob was made to feel welcome and comfortable. Despite his own political misgivings, he warmed to his prospective in-laws, and only hoped that Maggie would feel the same way about his parents.

He wasn't to be disappointed. He had warned his parents that he was bringing someone special home for lunch, and was taken aback, and not a little put out, that they showed no surprise at all. Maggie and his father were instantly taken with each other, and each seemed to bounce off the other. His mum was very impressed by Maggie's forthright nature and open way of communicating. In the few brief moments he was able to tear his eyes away from his bride-to-be, he noticed his mother looking at them both with warmth in her eyes. If he had had any doubts remaining about his impending nuptials they were dispelled that afternoon.

Within six months Maggie and Rob were celebrating their, unfortunately very short, honeymoon in Pemberton at the Karri Valley Resort. Their hotel room had a balcony that sat out over the lake and the few lights reflected beautifully off the water. On their first night they had watched a young couple canoeing on the lake, the young man had spontaneously burst into song – 'God knows I've fallen in love…'

They only had a few short days, as Parliament was sitting and the whip had been brutal in ensuring that Rob would be back to vote on some of the key issues that would be before the House over the next few weeks. They had promised each other that they would have a second honeymoon as soon as they had time. But the truth was that those few days had been absolutely perfect, following an almost event-free wedding, which in Rob's family was nothing short of a miracle.

Chapter Three

It had seemed that life couldn't possibly be better, but upon his return Rob discovered that part of the reason the whip had been so difficult about the length of his honeymoon was that there was to be a reshuffle, and Rob suddenly found himself Minister for Aviation. He was beside himself: how was it possible he could be a Minister already? Maggie was really proud of him, and even his new father-in-law seemed suitably impressed.

Of course, with the promotion came more hours and, although he hadn't thought it physically possible, more papers to read and letters to sign. Rob took his new responsibilities seriously, and not simply because he was an ambitious new Minister but because he was aware of how important air safety was to people, especially Australians. Being such a big country, Australia was dependent on air travel and freight. Thousands of Australians relied on air travel for business and pleasure, and Rob was going to make sure that they could do so in safety. Largely, Australia's air safety was recognised worldwide as being of a very high standard, but Rob knew that there was room for improvement, and it was his job to make sure that spending on air safety was not reduced in favour of the many other worthy areas that Government had a strong interest in. Of course he sometimes found this quite difficult, as he was committed to many other areas of Government expenditure; but he reminded himself that air safety was a life and death issue for Australians, and that kept him focused.

Rob started off as a new Minister with the same optimism as every other new Minister in any Government, sure that he could solve the problems in his portfolio if he was just committed, clever and hard working. However, despite the many, many hours he toiled with his Political Advisors and Civil Aviation officials, he realised that he could not possibly get across all of the issues he needed to in the time available. As it was, he was spending no time at all with his new wife, getting very few hours' sleep and even fewer meals.

Rob realised quickly that the people with the answer to any difficulties the CAA was facing were those that were working at the coalface. He spent time in local CAA offices speaking to those who were involved in regulating pilot licences and aircraft maintenance, ignoring those who suggested that this was overkill. He and his advisors spent considerable time meeting with these very impressive people who ensured Australia's status as one of the leading countries in the world in terms of air safety. They taught him the key issues in relation to ensuring air safety and maintaining it. Rob confirmed his own initial sense that much of this high level of air safety in Australia was down to awareness, resources and training; but the CAA staff provided him with some very practical methods to make it happen effectively.

This ministerial position was to teach Rob a very valuable lesson for the future. He realised quickly that it wasn't reasonable to expect Ministers to know everything about their portfolios. He knew that he could rely on his political and departmental advisors for strategic advice. However, he needed practical solutions to problems on the ground, and to check that CAA had the resources to ensure that no person could fly a plane or allow a plane to be flown until all regulations were met. It was crucial that everyone involved in air travel in Australia realised that heavy punishment would result for any breaches of safety requirements.

In his determination to succeed in his first ministerial post Rob did not notice the danger signs for his marriage, signs that workaholics often miss. Maggie, knowing how important this job was to Rob and being incredibly proud of his initiatives, made enormous efforts to support him and to make their limited time special. She knew from growing up living with her father how difficult it was to balance a political career and a home life, and secretly knew that her own job did not help the situation. She was now an advisor to the Shadow Minister for Health and her own hours and pressure was unenviable. Increasingly she was coming to see that both of them working at such a high level on opposite sides was having a negative impact. The person whom each wanted to confide in most was out of bounds on work-related issues.

Maggie missed her husband badly, and felt guilty that she regretted they had had such a short time as a newly married couple before his first ministerial post had come along. She was also feeling that, despite her previous commitment to the Liberal Party, she didn't like being on the opposite team to her husband. For her a period of reconsideration was underway, and yet her most important confidant hadn't even noticed. As a moderate, philosophically, in her own party, Maggie did not often disagree with her husband's ideals; it was methods they often disagreed on, though truth be told both had often had to concede (even if only privately) that each had fair points in defending their own proposed methods.

It wasn't that Rob didn't miss his wife – he did. He was just overwhelmed with the immense responsibility he had on his shoulders, and with the desperate need to make a success of it so that he didn't let down those who had supported him to get the ministerial position. He often felt isolated when he was confronted with enormous decisions, and worried he only received political and practical advice from the people around him, not the ethical advice he often felt he needed. Sometimes, by making some of the decisions asked of him he felt he was writing 'the world according to Rob Connor' and he didn't always feel 100% confident that he was making the right decisions. At these times he simply asked himself whether he had made the best decision he possibly could based on the information he had available to him at the time, and whether he had sought advice from the broadest base available to him. In public, as was expected of a Minister, Rob defended his views with 110% confidence. The Opposition and media would have ruthlessly exploited any hesitation on his part.

It was in the midst of this turmoil that the new Connor decided to make an early entrance. Maggie had started to be a touch snappy and looked very tired. Rob was extremely worried about her and suggested that she take some time off, a suggestion that was knocked on the head with all of his wife's characteristic forthrightness. He decided that it was simply overwork, and their lack of time together that was responsible for her fatigue. Maggie was worried: she had always been able to do long hours at work, have very little sleep and still manage to feel energetic. Lately, however, she had felt extremely tired, headachy and even nauseous. She had decided that it was all in her head and just got on with her busy life; but once she had gone off coffee, being the long-term coffee addict that she was, she felt this to be the first symptom to give her real cause for concern. After nagging from her mother, who didn't like how tired her daughter was looking, Maggie finally went to see her family doctor.

Dr Albert was a kindly old soul whom Maggie had not seen since her tonsils were taken out when she was twelve. He was a little concerned to see her, as he knew that she was normally a very healthy person. She explained to him that she had probably been overdoing it and it was nothing a little time off couldn't fix, but her mother had insisted that she make an appointment with him. Fortunately – or unfortunately, depending on how one looked at it – Dr Albert was not going to let Maggie leave his office with the normal lecture for overworked people, until he had fully checked her out. She was pale, and it was very unusual for even the most stressed people to experience nausea as one of their symptoms. He asked her a long list of standard questions, one of which related to the possibility of pregnancy. Maggie just laughed and said that Rob and her didn't get enough time together to make babies, immediately feeling embarrassed at her outburst in front of this older man. Dr Albert laughed in return and said that it was always a good idea to test her for pregnancy, if only to eliminate it. Maggie shrugged and obediently headed off to the toilets for the obligatory urine-in-a-bottle test.

She came back to his office and Dr Albert slipped out. When he came back he was looking a touch uncomfortable. Maggie waited expectantly wondering what weird and wonderful test he wanted her to do next, which he was clearly less than excited about discussing with her.

He cleared his throat and said, 'Maggie I am not sure how you are going to feel about this… but you are definitely pregnant.'

She stared at him for several seconds, unable to absorb the highly unexpected news.

'*I can't be!*' she declared when she had recovered somewhat. 'I think you had better test it again.'

'I have tested it three times, Maggie dear,' he replied quietly. 'I'm afraid that these little people do tend to come along in their own good time.'

Maggie closed her eyes, trying to get a handle on what she had just been told. A baby, she thought, what the hell am I going to do with a baby?

Dr Albert provided Maggie with advice on what she should and could not eat and drink, food supplements and reminded her that she could, and in fact should, come back to speak to him about being pregnant if she wanted or needed to. She would need scans within a few weeks to determine exactly how far pregnant she was, and that all was well.

Maggie left in a daze, not sure where to go. Rob was in a meeting when she got home and she wasn't sure what to do. Her mother resolved that issue for her by 'just happening' to be driving past on her way home, despite having to go a good twenty minutes out of her way to do this. Maggie laughed and let her in, grateful that she did not have to be alone with her news any longer.

Ingrid abstained from questioning Maggie about her doctor's appointment for the entire two minutes it took for her to make a coffee; a remarkable achievement.

'Not having one?' her mother asked surprised, knowing only too well her daughter's penchant for caffeine. A suspicion started to form at the back of her mind but she couldn't quite get it out; there was once a time that she herself went off coffee. When was that? she asked herself.

'Nah, don't really feel like it,' Maggie answered, seating herself outside in the small courtyard.

Her mother joined her and then, unable to wait any longer, she asked Maggie what had happened with Dr Albert, deeply concerned by now that her daughter was keeping something serious from her.

'Aaah,' Maggie sighed deeply, not quite sure how to approach telling her this news. She was still unclear how she felt about the idea of being a mother at this stage in her life. She was so used to planning and controlling most things before they happened. The patter of tiny feet before she was ready... well, they were entirely another matter. She took a deep breath and spluttered, 'It seems that I am pregnant.'

'Oh right,' her mother replied, 'Oh well it will be all right – sorry, *what did you say?*'

'I'm pregnant,' mumbled Maggie, her amusement at her mother's reaction temporarily lifting her spirits.

Ingrid sprang to her feet and dove over to her daughter, pulling her into her arms for a huge hug. Despite herself Maggie really had to laugh.

'I am going to be a grandma. *I am going to be a grandma!*' her mother danced around the courtyard. Then she looked up, serious now, and said, 'I have to go now and tell *everyone*.'

'I haven't had a chance to tell my husband yet,' Maggie said. 'You might want to put that on hold for a little while.'

'Yes, yes,' her mother said distractedly. 'Oh – so how are you feeling?'

Misunderstanding her mother's question about her state of health, Maggie launched into a confused and confusing monologue about whether having a baby at this point in her life was a good idea.

Her mother sat down, deflated. 'You mean that you might not have the baby? I mean, that is your right and you have worked hard on your career...' She trailed off.

'Oh, I don't know, Mum, it was just such a shock and I am so tired I don't know what to think. We were planning on having children but I didn't really think that it would happen for a few years yet. We both seem to have so much to do already,' said Maggie, not yet prepared to admit that she really hadn't been enjoying her work lately anyway and had been starting to think about what she would do next. Mother Nature seems to have made the decision for me, she thought, a touch bemused.

After further discussion, and some love and attention from her mum, Maggie saw her mother off and, feeling little better, waited for Rob's return. She didn't have long to wait, as he wandered through the door about fifteen minutes later. He came over to her and took her in his arms, sighing tiredly.

'What shall we do for dinner?' he asked. 'Shall I make us a salad?'

'Do you mind if we sit down and talk for a minute?' Maggie replied.

Rob looked surprised and then led her to the couch quietly. When they sat down she noticed his concerned look and decided to put him out of his misery.

'It seems,' said Maggie slowly, 'that we are pregnant.'

Rob's face was a picture. He seemed to stay still for an infinity, and Maggie thought her heart may have momentarily stopped beating. She watched his face as it hit him that he was going to be a father and he jumped up, pulling her into his arms and yelling, 'I am going to be a dad!' The pure joy on his face was exactly what Maggie had needed to see. She realised in that moment that she was pleased she was having a baby, but had been very concerned that Rob would be upset about the timing.

Her eyes filled with tears and Rob asked her, 'Aren't you happy about it, my love?'

She nodded, temporarily unable to speak. He sat back down on the couch with a thump, trying to come to terms with the news and his wife's reaction.

That night Rob and Maggie ordered in Italian food and sat in the courtyard to discuss their soon-to-be little person.

For the next few days they were both on a high, and continued to discuss how their incredibly busy lives would cope with a baby included. Rob was very surprised and, if he was honest, not a little relieved that Maggie wanted to give up her job. He knew how much her work meant to her and how hard she had worked to get where she was, and he would have hated her to have to give it up because she was forced to – even for a short time.

The next few months went along as usual, with far too much work and far too little sleep for both of them. They spent their rare spare time discussing where they would put a nursery, not that in their small cottage that needed too long a discussion, as there were only two spare rooms and one was already being used as a study. They discussed parenthood, names and what they thought their offspring would look like. Their biggest question was whether it would be a boy or a girl. Neither really cared – it sounded clichéd, but they just wanted a healthy, happy baby with all of its fingers and toes.

Maggie and Rob were both very nervous about being parents, but both sets of their own parents reminded them that this was how everybody felt when they were expecting their first child and they would be fine.

Maggie found to her own surprise that, far from being unhappy to leave her job, she was impatient to get time at home to set up for the now very large, uncomfortable and active bump in front of her. She had a rousing send-off from her colleagues, who she could tell were completely bemused by her decision to leave work to stay at home with the baby. She reminded herself that only seven months ago her job had been the centre of her universe as well, she would have been equally confused by such a choice by one of her colleagues. It was her that had changed, she thought ruefully, not them.

On 18 May, and some very long weeks after Maggie had wanted it to happen, Jack Joseph Connor was born. He was a perfect little boy with ten fingers and ten toes and a loud, hearty cry. Both parents were relieved to discover that they loved their little boy on sight.

Within days the little family were settled into the Pemberton Street cottage. Jack seemed happy in his little yellow room. Maggie was exhausted after the ten-hour labour but was completely fascinated by her son. Although nervous, the new parents had both managed to get through Jack's first nappy, first bath and his first feed with relative ease. They had both had very little sleep and were overwhelmed by their families' gifts, which had included a nappy service. The nappy service was to be the most inspired gift they received and quickly proved a life-saver.

Rob booked four weeks off work and thoroughly enjoyed his time with his little family, although he did feel as though he was going back to work for a rest. Work quickly absorbed enormous amounts of his time, and time at home inevitably involved interrupted sleep. Maggie was amazing, he thought. Every night her sleep was disturbed, but she seemed to remain calm, even when Jack was exercising his surprisingly loud voice. Their lives were still very busy, but Rob noticed that Maggie, although tired, seemed very engaged in her new role and really didn't seem to miss her political work. In fact in his quiet moments he was envious of Maggie being able to spend time with Jack every day and, in fact, of Jack being able to spend everyday with Maggie.

He had begun to notice changes in his wife that he had not expected. She was somehow more relaxed and calm than she had been when she worked in

Parliament House. She seemed content with what she was doing, and while he knew that she would eventually want to go back to some sort of work or study, he could see that she would never take up what she had been doing before she had Jack.

1987 saw another election, and Rob battled through this experience with limited sleep. Luckily, a swing to the Government, thanks to the popularity of the PM, ensured that Rob was returned as the Federal Member of Wilson. Rob returned to Canberra and was informed that he was to be Minister for Defence. This was his first Cabinet post and he was ecstatic. Defence was a serious Cabinet position, and he knew that the PM and his most senior colleagues must think highly of him to have promoted him to this office.

It was time, he knew, to review his staffing situation. He needed a senior advisor he could rely on to make sure that the quality of advice he had for making decisions was as good as he could get. As with his previous portfolio, Rob took his position very seriously; he knew that it was his job to ensure that Australia was well defended in any emergency and to keep its troops well trained in case they had to take part in any events overseas, peacekeeping or otherwise.

After putting his feelers out for some good advisors he was really pleased to hear that Gary O'Brien would consider a Senior Advisor's post. Gary had been a speech writer and political commentator in and around Parliament House for more than fifteen years. He was an old hand and had an excellent relationship with other Ministers and the press corps. Rob was determined to convince him to take the post and recommend some other staff for his fledgling office as well. He would keep his other advisors on but he knew that they were not up to this new role without significant guidance.

Gary arrived in his office at 9.30 a.m. and Rob met him at the door. His office was, as yet, devoid of a receptionist. He had tried to get his advisors to take turns to look after the front office, but they were so hopeless dealing with enquiries and phone calls that he had given up.

Gary was a tall man with a moustache and beard, and gave off an aura of being so laid-back that nothing would ever bother him. His sardonic answers amused Rob and he knew very quickly that Gary was the person who would kick his office into shape for him.

One week later, Gary was firmly at the helm. He had employed Sarah, a very competent receptionist, begun to allocate responsibilities to each of the advisors, and let Rob know that he needed an advisor to be based in Perth.

Rob hadn't realised how relieved he would be when Gary began to ensure that everything was running smoothly, and how crucial it was to have senior staff whose expertise and advice he could depend on. He was also pleased that he would have a ministerial office in Perth, as it would mean that he would be able to spend more nights at home.

Gary flew to Perth with him a few weeks later and

started looking around for a new advisor. The new member of the team would have to be someone established and able to spend considerable amounts of time working in isolation. Reg, from his electorate office, was keen for this new position and made his interest known to Rob. But Rob was uneasy; since Reg had started in his electorate office Rob had become aware that he was doing very little of the constituent work he had been employed to do. Rob was unsure exactly what he did do with his time, but he did seem to be engaged in a lot of party activities and appeared to be shoring up his own personal support within the party.

Gary's response was a resounding 'No'. He was quite forthright in his assessment that Reg was neither clever, competent nor committed enough for this new role. Rob was relieved that his own assessment had been supported. Although he still could not be swayed enough to get rid of Reg from his electorate office, much to the aggravation of the remainder of his office staff.

Gary rang him some days later to let him know that he had met the perfect person. Rob hastily arranged to meet this prospective candidate, Steve, at his newly organised ministerial office in Exchange Plaza in the centre of Perth city. Rob was impressed when he arrived at Exchange Plaza; his new office had a great view of the city. He was looking out over the Swan River from what would be his new workplace, surrounded by boxes, when the sound of voices alerted him to the fact that Gary and Steve had arrived. Steve was entirely opposite to Gary, a quiet man who considered each question fully before answering. He was clearly intelligent and Rob noted that his eyes missed nothing. Frankly, Rob had determined that if Gary thought he was the man for the job, then Rob would agree; but he was pleased as he realised that this was another person he felt sure he would work extremely well with.

Several months later, though extremely busy and under pressure with his new portfolio, Rob was gratified to see that his office was working like a well-oiled machine, and he felt strongly that the quality of the decisions and policy development coming out of it reflected this change.

In 1988 all residents of Parliament House were to move over to the new Parliament House building. Rob and his team were settled reasonably quickly in their new premises in the Ministers' 'wing' of the building. They were stunned by the room they had to occupy; Rob was equally impressed with his own office. After 'old Parliament House', this place was incredibly luxurious.

While Rob had loved the old Parliament House, he found the new building breathtaking. All of the wood and marble in the massive new building was taken from different parts of Australia. He couldn't put his finger on exactly what it was, but the new Parliament House building was quintessentially Australian. He loved it.

Life went on well for some time. Jack started producing teeth and shared his irritation and pain with all members of the family equally. When he started to walk, Rob was in Canberra and was disappointed with having to hear about this momentous occasion in a phone call. Maggie was relishing her role as Mum, especially now that Jack had started to talk. He was fascinating and very, very funny.

Despite this, and Rob's sadness about missing many of the milestones in his son's life, he had fallen into a pattern of allowing his work to encroach on the very small amount of time he had at home with his family. Many months went by without him seeing his mum or dad either. He wasn't aware that this was happening. It simply developed over a long period of time, as it does with most MPs who are not vigilant in protecting their personal time.

Chapter Four

The year 1990 saw a further Federal Election, and Rob found himself having to work a great deal harder in his electorate for this one. The campaigning was extremely difficult to balance with his ministerial responsibilities, and once again he was reminded that he would not be able to do this without Gary and the increasingly impressive Steve. Steve had shown himself to be extremely adept at balancing State and Federal politics in Rob's favour.

However, his electorate office was another matter. While Eleanor and Jackie, the receptionist and diary secretary, were working their fingers to the bone, Reg – unsurprisingly – was not! He was so caught up in managing numbers that he hadn't dealt with several constituent enquiries for months. In fact, a number of constituents had rung to complain. If Rob was picking up the vibes correctly from his electorate office, it appeared that Reg was getting their young volunteers to handle even those very few matters he had decided to deal with. Although he was at the office for many hours every day, it had become increasingly clear that Reg was, in fact, doing very little with regard to his in-house duties. To add insult to injury, Reg had demanded a meeting with Rob. Rob met with him, somewhat annoyed that this 'meeting' had to happen in the middle of an election campaign.

'Come in, Reg,' he said, looking up from the huge pile of papers in front of him.

Reg walked in and sat down in one of the chairs on the other side of the desk.

'How can I help you?' Rob enquired, trying to keep the irritation out of his voice.

'I think you should make me an advisor,' the now not-so-young teacher informed him.

'And why, pray tell, would I want to do that?' Rob asked.

Reg proceeded to provide a convoluted explanation as to why Rob should make him an advisor. From what Rob could make out, Reg was arguing that because of his degree he was cleverer than the others, and his years of loyal service should entitle him the job.

Frankly, it was more than Rob could take.

'Reg I am not making you an advisor, you are not entitled to it and I haven't seen any signs of you being capable of such a position. In fact if you don't pick up your act over the next three months and start doing your bit in relation to constituent matters, then you will find yourself without an Electorate Officer position as well. From this point on, Eleanor will be your manager and will report back to me as to your performance. We will have a review meeting here in three months; you can organise that time with Eleanor.'

Reg was speechless and his face flushed an ugly red.

He started to say something and then thought better of it. He backed out of the room hastily.

Rob called Eleanor in and advised her of the nature of the discussion. Although she was concerned about having to manage Reg, he could see she was relieved that he had finally decided to tackle this situation head-on. Rob thought grimly to himself that this matter should have been dealt with several years before, and felt somewhat ashamed.

Thanks to his staff (well, most of them anyway) and his many volunteers, Rob won his seat with only a very small swing against him, unlike many of his colleagues who found themselves in marginal seats, and several who had found themselves jobless. Still, the Government had a majority in the House of Representatives.

Rob and his team went back to Canberra with only a very short time off for good behaviour. At least he had had a couple of lovely days with Maggie and Jack. Jack was a holy terror, and Rob felt another pang of resentment that he was missing watching him grow up. He had also begun to notice a change in Maggie, but as yet he couldn't quite make out what it was.

Canberra was a less comfortable place to be on their return. The Treasurer, Paul Keating, began making claims that there had been an agreement between himself and Bob Hawke that Bob would stand aside for him after the 1990 election. However, all signs were that Bob was in for the long haul. Keating, whom Rob had never been particularly close to, was an impressive Treasurer and a spectacular parliamentary performer, and he was angry. Rob was seriously concerned for his Government. The Hawke/Keating leadership team was regarded as pretty unbeatable, and Rob was annoyed that Keating would destabilise such a successful partnership.

In the middle of 1991 Paul finally challenged Bob, but Bob's supporters rallied and he maintained his position. However, this clearly didn't settle the matter. Paul Keating was not finished with him yet, despite being relegated to the backbench. Rob was unhappy and unsettled during this period. All members of the Labor caucus were starting to position themselves in terms of who they were going to support. Rob wasn't concerned with who he thought would help him up the proverbial ladder; he had always liked Bob, and had plenty of reasons for maintaining his strong loyalty. He was also unable to shake his annoyance that Paul would upset the unbeatable team for his own personal ambition.

On 19 December 1991, Bob was successfully challenged by Paul to become not only leader of the Parliamentary party but also Prime Minister. Rob was shaken to the core. Unable to prevent his emotions showing, he moved away from the rest of his colleagues as quickly as he could without making it obvious how upset he was. He had to walk past the press to return to his office, but simply ignored them, somehow managing not to let them see his distress. He reached his office and locked himself into the tiny washroom where, finally, the tears came. He cried as he had not for many, many years. His disappointment and heartbreak for his mentor washed over him, and for a moment he couldn't get his breath back. He sat himself down on the closed toilet lid and got himself back together, but it was a full ten minutes before he was able to turn around and look at himself in the mirror. He washed his face with cold water in an effort to appear more normal and finally, taking a very deep breath, walked back into his office.

Gary had clearly been keeping an eye out for his return, and asked Sarah to organise a coffee for them both. He walked through and closed the door after him; Sarah followed closely behind with two steaming cups of coffee, seeming to understand when for the very first time Rob did not look up to thank her.

Gary sat silently sipping his coffee waiting for when Rob was ready to speak. Finally Rob sighed and said, 'I never thought that this would happen. I mean I knew he wouldn't be PM for ever, but I can't imagine what it will be like now he is gone.' His voice broke and he stopped again.

Gary didn't say a word, knowing that Rob would continue when he was ready. Rob spoke for a long time and Gary listened. Finally Rob felt able to face the world again. Gary advised him that he should handle the media by advising them that, while he was disappointed, he would throw his support behind the new Prime Minister. He said it was inevitable that the new PM would want to reshuffle his Ministers, and Rob might suffer from not having supported Paul in his bid.

Gary left, and Rob suddenly realised that he hadn't called Maggie. She would be waiting on hearing how the challenge had gone. He called her, and as he had thought, she was waiting by the phone for his call. She was shocked and really sad for Bob and for him. He could tell by her voice that she really understood how bad he felt, even if she had not really felt the same about Bob as he had.

The press calls had started coming in thick and fast, and Gary had drafted a press statement from Rob to be distributed. They were both amused to see that some of the younger staff were agitated, clearly wondering if their careers would suffer from the indignity of their Minister backing the wrong horse. No doubt they were keeping their ears open for new jobs in the event that their Minister lost his portfolio.

Rob put a call in to Bob's office, but was not surprised that he was not taking calls as yet; he knew Bob would call back when he had time to breathe. He thought again about how difficult it would be for Bob and Hazel to clear out of the Lodge, and his office, to make way for Paul Keating. Rob realised that his grief was moving steadily on to anger, he would have to carefully control these emotions in public, as the press would be looking closely for any signs of discontent amongst Hawke supporters.

Within hours, rumours were rife about what the new PM's Cabinet would look like. Rob didn't have long to wait. The next day the PM's office rang to say that Rob was going to be Minister for Employment,

Education and Training in the new Cabinet. Rob smiled grimly as he told Gary and Steve, who had flown over from Perth for moral support. Employment was the poisoned chalice, and clearly punishment for supporting Bob so publicly in the challenge. However, as Gary pointed out, it could be worse: he could have been out of the Cabinet altogether.

Steve suggested that Rob fly home to his family for a long weekend, there was no particular reason for him to be in Canberra right now. Rob agreed, as he felt completely exhausted. He had spoken to Bob that morning and all the grief and anger had come back to him in a rush. Bob had tried to be positive, and even joked about how he could now spend more time at the races; but it was clear that he was really bruised and battered and just putting on a brave face.

Rob flew back to Perth with Steve, who was great company and gave him a lot of space to be alone with his thoughts. As he walked through the front door to his cottage that evening he was filled with an amazing sense of calm. Maggie was sitting up waiting for him, curled up on the couch reading a book. She looked up as he walked through the door and held her arms open for him to join her. He dropped his bags and walked over to her and she held him for a long time while the tears fell. Soon there were none left and he sat back and told her what had happened. She made him a cup of coffee and they talked for hours. At one point he just stopped and looked at her for a long moment.

'What are you looking at me like that for, Rob?' Maggie asked, a touch confused by his sudden silence.

'I have missed you so much,' he said, gazing at her and taking her face in both of his hands, realising for the first time the true cost of his job.

Maggie's eyes filled with tears as she replied, 'Me too... oh, me too.'

That weekend was the happiest time the Connor family could remember in ages. Although Rob was still hurting about the treatment of his old friend, he thoroughly enjoyed the time he spent with his family and he made a vow to himself that he would never again allow his job to take over his family life. It was not going to be easy, given his ministerial responsibilities, but with a will there had to be a way.

Maggie and Rob invited both sets of their parents over for a barbecue and the cottage was filled with happy sounds. Even Maggie's father proved himself to be very understanding about the events of the previous week, and earned a new respect from Rob.

When he returned to Canberra the following week to meet with Departmental officials from the Department for Employment, Education and Training (DEET), he advised Gary straight away that he wanted to employ a further Senior Advisor to assist in the office. He made it clear, however, that Gary was his Chief of Staff, and that the reason for this change was because he needed to spend more time with his family. Gary, although not one to show his feelings to anyone, concurred that this was a sensible approach and let Rob know that he wished he had taken preventative methods such as this with his own family, as his marriage had broken up several years before, and he was now, at best, a weekend dad. Steve was also supportive, as he was very close to his family and invested enormous efforts in making sure it worked.

While knowing that this portfolio was the kiss of death in terms of senior ministerial portfolios, because of the large number of unemployed in Australia, Rob found himself immediately interested and involved in his new job. It was at this time that he realised that education and employment were very important policy areas, and so grew a strong interest he was to keep for his entire political career.

As he had done in his first ministerial job, Rob met with the people – DEET officials and others involved in employment, education and training at the coalface. This included academics and those working for the voluntary and community sector. Some seemed to be surprised that the Minister wanted to hear their ideas before he started to develop policy. In years to come, Rob would tell the story that he once went to a meeting of officials making policy in this area, and he became aware that only two of these officials had ever even met an unemployed person, and only one had been into a Commonwealth Employment Service (CES) office.

Within a few short weeks Gary and Steve had found Matt, a very tall, thin man with a quiet manner, to act as his new Senior Advisor. Matt was a whiz on Labor

Party workings and policy. Getting him was a coup for Rob, especially as he had clearly taken a step down the ladder since the new PM had started.

Despite himself, Rob had been impressed by the new PM's performance. As per usual his parliamentary performance left the Opposition gasping for air. His approach to his Cabinet colleagues' portfolios was vastly different to his predecessor's. He was very hands on, having clearly considered Bob's hands off approach a serious weakness. Rob could foresee future problems, with Cabinet Ministers being likely to object when Keating interfered in their areas of work. However, he had to admit that he was a formidable and competent Prime Minister. He was to maintain this new respect for Keating for the rest of his life. Although he kept it quiet he had even come to like this man who he would later say had been one of the country's best ever Prime Ministers.

Life was going very well at home as well. Rob had succeeded in spending most weekends at home, and Eleanor had been a great help in ensuring that nothing was ever booked for Sundays, unless it was extremely urgent. His parents were pleasantly surprised at how much they got to see their son, and were relieved that he had pulled back from his work before any serious damage was done to his marriage. They thought the world of Maggie and were impressed by her capacity to keep her family running with very little input from her husband.

Clearly, however, his input was reasonably significant, as within a few months Rob and Maggie invited their parents for lunch to let them know that they were pregnant again. Seven months later, Samantha was born, and she was beautiful. Even Jack, who had been more than a bit sceptical about this new arrival, was quite taken by the little person who had come to live with them.

It was during this period that Rob's patience ran out with Reg. He had fallen back into his lazy ways after a few very short months of substandard activity. Rob had given Reg several warnings and finally, after detecting the frustration of his other Electorate Officers, and in particular Eleanor, Rob decided the time had come to give him a final warning. He called him into his office one Friday and reminded him that his role as an Electorate Officer was to deal effectively with constituent matters. He advised him that the feedback from his manager was that he was not handling such matters at all, let alone dealing with them effectively.

'This is your last chance, Reg. If you intend to stay working here then you will need to get your act together. I will be checking on your progress every week and if your performance falls back one more time, you will be asked to leave,' Rob advised him.

Reg was furious and it showed. However, he clearly thought better of letting Rob know what was on his mind. The following week Rob received Reg's resignation, as he had been offered a position with one of the unions. Rob could not help but sigh with relief; he was aware that one of his failings was not being able to deal firmly with his staff. He was grateful for most of his team, who operated from a sense of professional commitment and pride, and therefore did not require his intervention; though the crisis had passed he knew that he could not remain this lucky for ever.

It was only a few short months before Rob found himself in the midst of another election campaign. This one was cause for concern. The public had not had a chance to pass judgment on Paul Keating, and if the polls were anything to go by it was unlikely to be pretty. There was a great deal of trepidation in the Party about facing this election. Unfortunately, Keating's previous job as Treasurer didn't help as he was still seen as the 'taxman', a role not best-loved by the people.

His advisors and electorate staff got together, minus their departmental colleagues, to ensure that they planned the campaign period carefully. Rob had spent every moment he could spare over the past twelve months knocking on doors in his electorate. But he was only too aware that being a Senior Cabinet Minister did not leave him much time to be a particularly good local MP. He was aware that being the Minister responsible for employment might cause a backlash from people who felt he should be doing more. He had always maintained at least two Fridays a month in his electorate office meeting constituents and community groups. He was also aware that since Reg had left his electorate office, the staff was doing a much better job at dealing with constituent issues. Reg's replacement, Naomi, was dynamic and efficient.

Constituents warmed to her optimism and she was unyielding with Departments and other organisations who had made mistakes in their dealings with Rob's constituents. He was glad that he had made this change for other reasons as well; the electorate office was a brighter, friendlier place since Reg had moved on.

Maggie, despite being a new mum, threw herself into this election campaign, and it was not unusual to see them knocking on doors together. Maggie charmed people with her capacity to communicate with them, and often the door-knocking took a very long time. They were greeted well, even by those who clearly indicated that they didn't plan to vote for Rob. He in turn appreciated their honesty and enjoyed passing the time of day with them.

Endless hours of stuffing envelopes, letterbox dropping, door-knocking and walking through local shopping centres filled their time quickly. Both sets of their parents were happy to babysit whenever it was needed, and sometimes the kids would come and spend time at the office, when Rob and Maggie were going to be there to keep an eye on them. Jack and Samantha seemed quite at home in the bustling environment of the office.

This election was important to Rob, as John Hewson, the new Opposition Leader, was planning the introduction of a Goods and Services tax. The Labor Party, not surprisingly, was totally opposed to it. Such taxes in other parts of the world had not worked as effectively on broadening the tax base as Hewson would have the electorate believe, and in many countries they had realised too late that reversing such a tax was near on impossible. The tax would clearly benefit those who, in percentage terms, spent less on groceries and necessities to live, and cause inordinate problems for those who were already spending most or all of their income to live. He was concerned that this would lead to families having to eat cheaper foodstuffs and cause health problems in the longer term. Ultimately, the cheapest way to eat would be bread and tinned food.

On the night before the election, when he had finally made it home to his family, Rob sat exhausted with his head in his hands and said to Maggie, 'The voters are going to vote Hewson in and they don't know what they are doing. A GST will break many of them.'

Maggie simply took his hand and led him into the bedroom, tucking him quietly in to bed and said, 'Darling, you have done everything you can now… Leave it up to the voters to decide what to do.'

Rob fell into a fitful sleep and woke at 4.30 a.m. to the sound of the alarm. Maggie was already up with Samantha, and he marvelled at how good she looked at such an awful time of the morning. Samantha was also bright and chirpy; well, she would be, wouldn't she? She had been the only one to get a full night's sleep.

Rob made breakfast and then told Maggie he was off to the office. He told her to go back to bed and just head down later on. Maggie said firmly that once Jack was up and they were all dressed and breakfasted she would be straight down there.

Rob went down to the office, making a few quick stops at polling booths along the way, where dedicated ALP volunteers and supporters were fast stealing the best positions for posters and how-to-vote cards, before their rivals arrived. They were pleased and surprised to see him, and he knew it gave them a boost to see him so optimistic when they fully expected to lose the election. Secretly he felt that they had no chance, but this was not the face he was prepared to let his supporters, or the press for that matter, see.

When Maggie arrived two hours later with Jack and Samantha in tow, Rob was having a quick coffee with his advisors and electorate office team, to discuss the latest polling. They had not stopped for the past two hours but Rob knew that this fifteen minutes was important to them all before the onslaught of the day really hit them. Maggie and the kids sat quietly with them while Rob said that whatever happened, they had done all that they could possibly do and it was up to the voters now. He thanked them for their enormously hard work and let them know that he knew that this was a big day for them too, as their livelihoods were also in the balance.

He looked around the room and saw that his staff were touched that he had thought about their situations at a time like this. He also received an amused smile from Maggie, who had obviously decided that she should be his speech-writer.

Then it was off, and running at a pace that would last for the next ten or twelve hours at least. The phones rang and rang with well-wishers, the media, those who did not want to well wish but to harangue, and polling booths frantically requesting assistance. Older and disabled voters had to be picked up and taken to polling booths to vote and then returned home. Rob was required to drive around to each of the booths to provide moral support and to answer the questions of those about to vote while he was there. He knew his presence helped the polling booth volunteers in what was a very difficult task. Voters could often be rude and abusive, many of them displeased about voting being compulsory. Maggie had taken on the job of taking food and drinks to polling booths for their volunteers, short respite on a blisteringly hot day.

Labor had suffered a humiliating defeat in the WA State elections only a month before, and Labor supporters could still taste the bitter pill in their mouths when they thought about it. The polls clearly showed that this was going to be a defeat as well. Rob admired their guts getting out there in the heat, taking abuse from voters despite knowing that they were about to get defeated.

When the polls closed the vast majority went to the community hall where there was a big television and refreshments to await the results. Rob stopped by to see them all before heading back to his office. He paused to speak to them and thank them before being dragged back to the car to speak to a radio station wanting his comments. Then he was whisked back to the office and the doors were closed while they awaited the results.

The wait was excruciating. The results coming in from his own polling stations were not as good as in previous elections, though he still seemed to be marginally ahead in most of the results. Tom Bennett was working frantically trying to record the polling station results and ascertain where Rob's vote was at.

'It's very close Rob – I just don't know if we're going to make it,' the quietly spoken Tom advised.

Maggie glanced at Rob with concern, but he managed to maintain an optimistic look on his face. At the first opportunity he managed to extricate himself and went to stand quietly in his own office. Maggie joined him a minute later and they held each other.

'It's okay,' he said, 'whatever happens it will be okay.' But neither of them were fooled by his words. His inner five-year-old was still there, desperate to be the Boss of Australia. Not only were they looking at losing Government, he might well lose his seat and his dreams along with it…

Gary joined them and said quietly, 'Rob you should come out and see this.'

Rob and Maggie joined the others in front of the small TV set in time to hear Bob Hawke claiming that the Labor Party had won the election. They shook their heads in disbelief; surely Bob was just being optimistic? But before they could turn their attention away, Bob Hogg, a senior Labor Party figure, was on making the very same claim. Hogg was a cautious man and unlikely to make such a claim unless he was quite sure. After a moment's silence as they came to terms with what had been said, the room exploded in cheers and tears. They had done the impossible – Keating had won the election!

Rob swung into action. He needed to get down to the community hall to his supporters and speak to them. The press were waiting for him outside his office but he refused to speak to them until he had spoken with those waiting at the hall. He forced his growing disquiet about his own job down inside himself and made his way up onto the small stage so he could be heard by everyone. His supporters waited, holding their breath.

'It appears as if we have done it, we have won the election. Wilson is not so sure at this stage. But remember this, it doesn't matter whether I have won my seat or not. We have won the election and saved Australians from the GST!' he claimed buoyantly.

His supporters raised a rousing cheer, and many were to comment after this moment that for the very first time Rob looked like a leader, like a man who could one day be Prime Minister himself. He had a statesmanlike quality that hadn't been seen in Australia for quite a long time.

A few minutes later on the big screen they could all hear the crowds at Keating's Bankstown electorate screaming, *'We want Paul!'*

A smiling Prime Minister came to the stage and said simply, 'Well, you've got me.'

The noise from the crowd was breathtaking. Keating went on to claim that this was the greatest victory of all. And who would argue? They had snatched victory out of the jaws of defeat. There would be no other election night like it.

The crowds celebrated for many hours, and the last stragglers were seen leaving the hall well after 4 a.m. the next morning. They had been up for nearly twenty-four hours.

Rob Connor had to wait nearly a week for the Electoral Commission to confirm that he had won his seat. He was sure that he had aged ten years during that week.

Chapter Five

Keating did another reshuffle after the '93 election and Rob found himself the Minister for Finance. This new position indicated that he was back in favour with the Prime Minister. It could also have meant that the Prime Minister was trying to butter up the ALP factions, for Rob had long been one of the few MPs who had cross-factional support.

The Minister for Finance position was challenging, and he realised that much of what people thought the Treasurer did was actually the domain of the Finance portfolio.

He kept nearly all of his staff on with only a few alterations due to the departmental liaison staff changing, because he had now to deal with the Department for Finance.

Gary had stayed, and Matt seemed in no hurry to move on. Steve was still keen to remain as his advisor in Perth, so all was well there. He would have hated to have changed staff at such a late stage and he knew from other Ministers that he was particularly lucky with his team. Many other Ministers had suffered badly because of their poor choice of staff, resulting in very poor advice.

He had an approach from a Mal Featherstone, who had offered his services, but only if Rob made him his

Chief of Staff. Rob was surprised by the arrogance of Mal's manner, given that he had previously stood against the Labor Party in an election. Rob knew that his senior team, headed by Gary, was a winner and he was at no time tempted by this audacious approach. He knew he needed to be completely sure of his team in this new ministerial post, so he thanked Mal for thinking of him, and wished him well.

This decision was to prove crucial. Heading for the 1996 election, Rob found himself in a surprising position. He hadn't noticed it but his quiet intelligence and developing statesmanlike approach to his work had been noticed by his colleagues. Many were becoming less impressed by Keating's brash approach to voters and the media. However, Rob had grown to really respect Paul while he had been PM, and was not keen to engage in any leadership speculation.

In 1995 Brian Howe, the very well respected Deputy Prime Minister and leader of the left faction of the Parliamentary Labor Party, decided to resign. He was not going to stand at the next election, and wanted to give his successor a chance to settle into the position of Deputy PM before the '96 election. Suddenly Rob found himself the subject of much conjecture. The Deputy PM position was usually a job earmarked for his left faction colleagues and so he had never considered himself to be in the running. However, to his great surprise it became clear that he was the chosen candidate of both factions. Within a few short weeks and with a very smooth transition, Rob was confirmed as the Deputy Prime Minister. He retained his Finance portfolio as well so life, particularly as it was a pre-election year, was extremely busy. He kept on his entire staff in his new position and also kept on a couple of Brian's staffers, including Catherine Reynolds. Cath was a particularly impressive, intelligent young woman, whom Rob had noticed when she had worked with Brian. She provided a valuable social policy background and complemented his own staff very well. Gary was particularly taken with her efficiency, Rob noted. Overall his team was shaping up very well.

Despite his overwhelmingly busy schedule, Rob continued to set aside two Fridays a month to see his constituents, and every Sunday was spent with his family. Maintaining this schedule was very difficult, particularly as Keating was a demanding boss. However, early on in their new relationship as PM and Deputy, Rob advised Paul that the reason for his decision not to work on Sundays was that he needed to spend quality time with his family. He was surprised when Paul immediately backed off, and it was then that Rob knew that the rumours about Paul being a family man were true. Rob wondered how he managed to balance his work and family life.

Samantha was growing into a lovely and lively little girl. She had just started school and he could see that Maggie was missing being able to spend so much time with her daughter. Jack was becoming a teenager and yet again Rob found himself regretting the lost time with the children. Both his offspring were remarkably well balanced, and he knew he had Maggie to thank for that. While most of their friends were enduring their children's early teenage years, Maggie and Rob were genuinely enjoying the smart, creative boy who was their son. Rob knew that Maggie needed to reconsider where she was at, now that she was not going to need to be a full-time mum.

One Sunday, Rob and Maggie were sitting on their lovely verandah and Maggie began to talk about what she was going to do with her life.

'I genuinely don't know what to do now,' she said to Rob, 'I don't really want to go back to what I used to do before. I need something where I can do flexible hours and still be available for the kids.'

'What about study or part-time work?' Rob suggested.

'I have been thinking,' she replied, 'No… it's stupid.'

Rob prompted her to say what was on her mind; he was sure that Maggie could do whatever took her fancy but he knew that she couldn't see that at the moment.

Maggie went on to tell him that she would really like to write books, children's stories. Rob was surprised, remembering the hard-nosed political advisor that his wife had been before Jack and Samantha had come along. Despite the change, though, he could see her being really good at writing books for children, as he had heard her make up stories at night to soothe their own children into sleep, and had been amazed by her impromptu creativity.

Their conversation went on to how she could do this, and the primary problem appeared to be the lack of space in their small cottage. Rob waited for his wife's solution to the difficulty, hoping that her answer wouldn't be to move to a bigger home. He had fallen in love with this cottage. He could see it was too small to cater for a study for her and wanted to find a way around it, but it would be a real wrench to leave it. He realised he had not been listening to what she was saying, and quickly computed that she was proposing building a second floor on the cottage. He agreed readily, immensely relieved that this was her proposal.

Over the next few weeks Rob was reminded of the old Maggie and her ruthless efficiency. She drafted plans that were sympathetic to the post-World War One structure, and the local Council had agreed 'in principle', provided the addition was identical to the plans.

Within four months the beautiful Pemberton Street cottage had a second floor, with a large bedroom, bathroom, walk-in wardrobe and a beautiful, spacious study that held room for Rob and Maggie to have their own work area. The second floor was almost as big as the lower floor and was beautifully completed. Rob's cousin, Warren – a real estate agent – said that he believed that the renovations had more than doubled the value of their property.

Maggie started to set herself up in her study. She took short creative writing courses and began a writer's journal, which she had been advised to do. Murdoch

University was offering two semesters in creative writing, and Maggie enrolled. It had been a long time since Rob had seen Maggie so enthused about anything to do with herself.

In the meantime Rob was doing well in his new position. He enjoyed the responsibility of stepping in as Acting PM when Paul was out of the country or on holidays. But the next election was coming up fast, and nobody in the Labor Party was under any illusions: they were not going to win the election.

After a difficult election campaign, the Party was not to be disappointed; they were trounced by Peter Gooring and his Liberal Party. Rob retained his seat and was quickly selected by his Parliamentary Party colleagues to lead the Party, after Paul decided that he no longer wanted to stay on in Parliament.

Rebuilding the Parliamentary Party after a devastating election defeat was Rob's first job. His biggest benefit was that he was surrounded by a well-qualified team of ex-Ministers for his Shadow Cabinet. With advice from his senior people he chose his Shadow Cabinet very carefully and managed to select what was generally regarded to be a formidable team. The new Gooring Government was a young bunch, and most of the new Ministers had never had ministerial experience. Early on, Rob's team made quite a few points which Gooring found hard to rebut.

Rob had no time for Gooring. He had lost respect for him during the election campaign, particularly as Gooring had played populist politics and encouraged intolerance amongst voters. Rob's pet hate was racism and discrimination, and he objected to the signs that Gooring was prepared to take advantage of the divisions in the community, caused by the temporary popularity of a right-wing party with extremely intolerant and simplistic views.

Gooring had left him with a very small staff in his office, but fortunately he didn't have to lose many people. Several who had worked with the Party since it assumed Government in 1983 had decided to take this opportunity to move on to other things. Gary had spoken with Rob about taking on some of Keating's staff who were keen to stick around. Rob, Gary, Matt and Steve met in Perth to discuss the best staff mix they could have. Finally they sorted it out, and offers were made and accepted before the day was out.

Rob found himself with an unexpected afternoon and evening off so he stopped in at the Re Store for a couple of mixed meat and cheese ciabattas and two lattes, and went home to surprise his wife.

He walked into the now not-so-little cottage with his cache and felt the stress of the last few months leave him. The cottage was filled with piped music, and lavender incense filled his nostrils. His home was the epitome of calm, a veritable haven from the outside world. He set the rolls and coffee down and went to find his better half. She was staring with great concentration at her laptop screen, reading what she had just written. She then sat back and smiled, clearly content with what she had produced. Getting a sense she was being watched she turned around and her face filled with surprise and pleasure at seeing her husband. He walked over and leant down to kiss her gently.

'To what do I owe this pleasure?' she asked.

Rob told her in brief what had happened that day, and then they both went downstairs and took their lunch out onto the verandah.

The afternoon passed slowly and calmly, and then their peace was shattered by a small girl who raced over to them from their neighbour's car. Samantha ran towards them, beside herself that both of her parents were sitting outside waiting for her. The neighbour waved and drove off. Soon they were all laughing and joking outside. Before long Jack was there too, and they all decided to head down to Fremantle for fish and chips on the pier. The kids changed and they loaded themselves into the car and headed down to Kailis. This was one of their favourite spots; they took their paper packets filled with steaming hot fish and chips loaded with salt and vinegar and sat on the esplanade. There were a lot of other families down there and the air was filled with laughter. Seagulls and flies swarmed around them but nobody minded. Maggie and Rob sat and watched while the kids played on the swings and slide. Well – Samantha played; Jack had clearly reached the age where he was too cool for such behaviour, so he just walked awkwardly around the play area, ostensibly to keep an eye on his sister. A few people recognised Rob and wandered over to say hello, but most respected his privacy and let him be.

It was a very content family that drove home that night. The kids showered and they all sat on the verandah in their PJs with a hot chocolate. Rob and Maggie both tucked Jack and Samanatha into bed that night. Then they went and sat on the couch and cuddled, listening to Pavarotti crooning in the background.

Chapter Six

Rob's period as Opposition Leader wasn't easy, but he was grateful for his experience as a Minister as this had prepared him well. However, he had never had his personal life and approach so open to public speculation before, and he found that very difficult. Suddenly his background, his marriage and even his children were fair game.

Rob had determined a leadership strategy with his senior advisors that suited his style. He was never going to adopt Keating's style of leadership; it would not have suited him and wouldn't have been his choice anyway. Rob had decided to stick with his normal style, which was not to be negative about everything the Government did. He would bide his time and then, when he did stand up on issues, the press would be sure to take notice. He had also chosen his Shadow Cabinet carefully based on their skills, experience and capability, and was going to adopt Hawke's more consensual style and not interfere in his Shadow Ministers' portfolios, unless pre-agreed.

The press were initially surprised that Rob and his team did not immediately jump on every mistake or policy change introduced by Gooring's Government. This was a hard position to maintain, as Gooring and his crew made repeated mistakes and their parliamentary performance was woeful. However, Rob's position was that this was a new team that needed to find their feet. He maintained if they made decisions that would be detrimental to the Australian people he would come down on them like a ton of bricks.

One issue that had become a real sticking point early on in his time as Opposition Leader was that of the 'Stolen Generation'. For some time now Australians had become increasingly aware of the fact that Government policy in the 1950s and beyond had resulted in many Aboriginal children being taken involuntarily from their parents. Many had never seen their parents again, and many had ended up doing menial work that was little better than slave labour. More and more information was becoming available about the devastating effects these policies had had on these families. A report and video about the experiences of the 'Stolen Generation' as they were known, was produced.

Rob and his team watched the documentary video, and there was not a dry eye in the room. Rob was palpably aware of the devastation that had been wreaked on these families because of blatantly discriminatory policies. He removed himself to read the lengthy report that had accompanied the video, and as he read about the pain and anguish the 'Stolen Generation' and their families and communities had experienced he felt a pain in the pit of his gut for what they had been through. He knew in that moment that the very least the Government should do would be to apologise for the policies that had led to the anguish of its own people. Surely the primary role of Government should be to protect its people – all of them.

It was to have a particularly devastating effect in his home town, where a highly respected and well-liked indigenous member of the community committed suicide in the aftermath of the report. Rob was mortified to think these policies could still be claiming victims and grieved at the loss of such an impressive community leader and friend.

He made contact with the Prime Minister's office the next day, feeling sure that the PM would want to make a public statement of regret that this had taken place, and thinking that as this was not a party political issue they could issue a joint statement. He was somewhat bemused at the run-around he got. However, nothing could have prepared him for the press release issued by the Prime Minister's office, stating that an apology could not be issued by the Government because it would open the floodgates for compensation.

Rob and his team were completely floored. Surely the Government could not be playing politics with a group of people, still suffering from being ripped from the arms of their families, often never to see them again? Surely an apology was not necessarily an expression of guilt or responsibility but an expression of regret for their pain and suffering? Rob wondered if he was being naïve, but he did not feel that compensation was the objective of those highlighting these dreadful practices. The objective appeared to him to be a desire for acknowledgement that the practices were wrong, and of the impact they had had on the 'Stolen Generation' and their families; a chance to heal the wound.

No amount of coaxing and negotiations would move the PM from his defensive position, but as Rob saw Premiers all over the country say 'Sorry' to the 'Stolen Generation' without the predicted floods of compensation claims, he vowed that his first act as PM would be to say sorry.

Life at home was going extremely well. Jack had hit his teens for real now, and had thoroughly surprised his parents by not becoming a hormone-led brat. Samantha was loving school – well, the social aspects of school anyway. Homework, it appeared, was simply a downer in an otherwise perfect life! Maggie and Rob tried everything to get her to do her homework: bribery, cajoling and even a little emotional blackmail. But Samantha's Taurus star sign shone through, and eventually Ingrid provided a brilliant piece of advice, which was to let Samantha take the consequences of her actions. Stick to their rules, which were that there would be no TV or going over to friends' houses unless she could demonstrate that she had completed her homework, and let her take the criticism from her teachers. An early lesson that all actions have consequences would not hurt the irrepressible Samantha. Rob and Maggie hated having to remove all the fun things in their daughter's life, but after a few hairy months Samantha finally got it and started doing her homework without being asked. How well she did it – well, that was another story; but Rob and Maggie left that to her teachers. Ingrid had received heroic status for her fabulous parenting advice, and Maggie and Rob resolved to run to her much earlier when the next problem arose, which it inevitably would.

Maggie had finished her two semesters at university and had thoroughly enjoyed them. Her tutor, Jim, had been very impressed with her work, especially with her amazing ability to write stories that would fascinate young children. For her coursework she had had to write in various styles, but writing in some of them had been hard and had caused her to stress and worry, whereas children's stories were fun for her and came easily. Jim had a friend whose partner worked for a leading publishing company and he gave Maggie the contact on her last day. When Rob got home that weekend, he found Maggie distracted and a little bit anxious. Finally, after repeated enquiries about what was bothering her, Maggie finally produced the card that Jim had given her. Rob was confused, 'I don't understand the problem, Maggie, just give him a call,' he said.

To his surprise Maggie's agitation increased, in direct proportion to Rob's confusion. 'I can't – what if he hates my work?'

'So what if he does?' Rob asked. 'Although I can't think that it is likely, given how much Jim liked it.'

Maggie paced the floor and Rob watched her in

wonder, this must be what they call 'the artistic temperament'. Suddenly he couldn't help himself, he burst out laughing, holding his sides. Maggie stopped and looked at him, horrified. The sight of him holding his stomach laughing was too much for her, she smiled, and soon she had joined him, with tears running down her face. The sound brought Jack and Samantha out from their bedrooms to the lounge where they stood gazing silently at their parents who, it appeared, had gone totally mad. Soon Maggie and Rob couldn't laugh anymore, as their stomachs hurt. When there was silence, Jack asked hesitantly, 'Ummm – what was so funny?'

Shaking their heads, Jack and Samantha left their hysterical parents laughing themselves into a stupor, having lost it again after their son's question.

Maggie and Rob finally recovered themselves and sat on the couch together. Neither really knew why they had dissolved into laughter but both knew that Maggie had been having a rare totally illogical moment.

'Aaahhh!' she sighed. 'It's stupid, isn't it? I've got to stop stressing myself about it. I just need to decide whether I'm going to approach him or not.'

'Yep,' replied Rob. 'I hardly think that Jim would use one of his personal contacts for someone he wasn't pretty sure would make it.'

'I hadn't thought of that,' Maggie said reflectively.

They discussed Maggie's approach for a while and then Rob had a sudden moment of clarity. He felt sure, for no reason he understood, that Maggie was suddenly very afraid of being successful. Writing children's stories was way out of her comfort zone. In political circles Maggie was well within her comfort zone but as an author she was breaking new ground, and this ground didn't feel quite as secure. He felt sure if she took some baby steps to start with then she would be fine; although a giant leap would work just as well.

Of course, Maggie made the phone call, and the Connor family lived on tenterhooks for the week and half before she met Jim's friend Paul and his partner, Jamie. Maggie met with them at their small terrace house in Fremantle. She couldn't fail to be impressed by the beautiful stone house, which was sympathetically decorated with jarrah floorboards, high ceilings and cornices. Paul met her at the door and took her through to the small courtyard. Jamie was a small, flamboyant man who was clearly at home in his surroundings. They chatted over several glasses of wine but Maggie found it unusually difficult to relax, despite the laid-back atmosphere. Finally, Jamie said, 'I hear from Paul that you are an author – and if the lovely Jim's view is anything to go by, you are damn good at it.'

Maggie flushed a deep red and found herself stammering, 'Well, I have written a few stories, but I well, well, umm…'

Paul and Jamie laughed, then Paul said, 'He also said that you had no sense of how good your work is.'

Maggie tried to laugh with them but found that she still could not relax until she knew that she hadn't embarrassed herself by contacting them.

Jamie and Paul continued to smile, amused by this woman sitting in front of them. Jamie already knew that Maggie had to be good, Jim had never imposed on their friendship before on behalf of one of his students, not in the last twelve years. Jamie and Paul knew him well enough to know that this one was good, even if she took some convincing about it.

Jamie finally said, 'Come on, Maggie, let's see what you've got.'

Maggie pulled her portfolio out and very tentatively handed it over, still concerned about putting something so personal and special to her on the line for judgment. Jamie took it and settled himself inside on the couch with his glass of wine. Paul took charge of Maggie, settling her back in the courtyard with a glass of fabulous Rioja and asking her about Jim. The two laughed at her stories of his unorthodox teaching methods, and some of the bizarre assignments he had set for his students. Every so often Jamie would chuckle or murmur at what he was reading. Maggie would look over obviously startled. Paul tried very hard not to smile at her obvious discomfort, at the needless agony she was putting herself through. He had an artist friend who specialised in still life, and she was the same every time she had a gallery showing.

Finally Jamie heaved himself up from the small couch, sighing as he refreshed his glass on the way back to the courtyard.

Maggie found herself watching his every move, trying to read meaning into it. Jamie was well aware that she was watching him carefully and could not help himself; he played up every gesture, knowing it was increasing her agitation. Part of him felt a bit bad, knowing what he had to tell her; another part was thoroughly enjoying the drama of the moment.

Finally he sat with the others at the chunky jarrah picnic table that Paul had 'rescued' from a second-hand shop in Hampton Road. He looked seriously at Maggie, consciously extending the moment, and said 'Maggie I have to tell you the truth about your work, it is my job to be completely honest.'

Maggie's heart sank. Well, it hadn't exactly started like a rave review, had it? Not that she had expected that kind of response, but she had hoped he would find just a few signs of talent hidden deep within the work. She held her breath as he prepared to deliver the verdict.

Jamie poured more wine into his glass and said, 'Maggie, it's great! Not good – *great*! The characters are fabulous, the scene is described so beautifully that I was captivated by it. It's new and original.'

Maggie just stared at him and Jamie and Paul couldn't help but laugh.

'You really liked it?' she replied in a small, choked voice.

'I loved it – it really is good. There are a few places that need a bit of tidying up, but that's just editing.'

Maggie grinned. 'The question is whether anyone will be crazy enough to publish it.'

Jamie looked serious now. 'Maggie, I would publish it, but you need to start thinking seriously now about whether you want a literary agent. We are large publishing firm and publish across a broad range of genres. You may decide to go with a publisher that specialises in children's books. Now is when you need to get serious about what is best for you. I am more than prepared to give you some contacts that may help you, but you need to do some research and decide what you want.'

Maggie was only half listening at this point. Not only had Jamie told her that her work was good, he had told her he would publish it. She had worked in politics too long; she needed someone to be prepared to put their money where their mouth was before she would believe them.

They talked for another hour or so and then Maggie felt that she had imposed on them too long. She had really taken to Paul and Jamie and felt strongly that they would wind up being friends. They each kissed her goodbye warmly and, after exchanging contact details, asked her to stay in touch and call them should she need anything.

On the way home Maggie felt as though she needed to pinch herself. In her wildest dreams she had not imagined that Jamie would like her work so much that he would offer to publish it. She arrived home quite late and was gratified to see that the lights were still on. She found Rob sitting quietly reading through some work papers, with a glass of red by his side. He looked so lovely right at that moment, she thought, his face slightly screwed up as he concentrated on what he was reading. She walked through and sat down beside him.

'Watcha up to?' she asked.

He looked over to her and smiled, putting his papers down beside him.

'How did it go?' he asked eagerly.

'I'll tell you once I've made myself a cuppa… want one?' she said.

'No, and neither do you until you tell me,' he said, pulling her close so that she could not escape to the kettle.

'Well,' she said, 'Jamie liked my work, so much in fact that he said that he would be prepared to publish it.'

Rob grinned and hugged her tightly, 'I knew he would, how could he not – it's great!'

She looks so beautiful, he thought to himself, her face is radiant. He pulled her as close as he could manage on the awkward couch and kissed her passionately on the lips. She sighed deeply, moulding herself into his arms. Soon all thoughts of books and publishing offers were put out of their mind. Rob took her hand and led her up to their new bedroom overlooking the city. It was very late the next morning by the time they came down for breakfast.

Jack and Samantha groaned loudly at the two of them gazing at each other and giggling at everything the other said.

'They are so gross,' Jack mumbled.

For once his sister agreed with him, and they left their parents there while they walked down to the deli for an ice cream. Rob and Maggie didn't even notice they were gone.

While things were going really well at home, Rob was finding Opposition extremely difficult. He had determined not to simply oppose everything the Government did, but their policies were so appalling he found it difficult not to criticise their every move.

One issue the Government had chosen to taken a hard line on was refugees. Rob agreed that the intake of refugees should be managed and that they should be screened, as anyone coming into Australia should be. However, he could not believe the unfair treatment refugees were getting at the hands of this administration.

Justice certainly wasn't this Government's strong suit. Within a very short time of winning the election, the Gooring Government had decided to 'reform' the administrative review tribunals. Not many Australians knew much about these tribunals, until they needed them, of course. Rob, as lawyer, knew that these tribunals were the best in the world and that they dealt with all the issues that affected Australians on a daily basis: tax, social security, employment and education. The Government's plans soon became clear. They intended to remove people's right to have their say in a hearing in front of a tribunal judge, and to remove people's right to have someone to represent them. Their excuse was that the tribunals were too expensive. Rob felt sure that justice was too important to come down only to dollars and cents.

The Government was taking a hard line on social security recipients, blaming unemployment on those who were unemployed. The term 'dole bludger' raised its ugly head again. Yet Rob knew that the figures showed that for every one job there were nine unemployed people.

Rob felt a growing sense of unease as the Government appeared to manipulate people into believing that the answer to all of these problems was simple; that all that was needed was a hard line taken against those allegedly abusing the system to protect the public purse.

The public appeared to take to these ideas like a duck to water. Newspapers and chat shows were filled with people hailing the Government's paternalistic approach as the way to solve the country's ailments. Rob and his team felt deflated. Was this what they were going to have to do to win power?

The Minister responsible for social security payments introduced targets for officials to meet on social security fraud. All of a sudden Rob and his colleagues found their electorate offices inundated with social security matters where the Department had wrongfully claimed that people had received monies they were not entitled to. Some regional offices were fine and corrected the mistake as soon as it was pointed out. Some, however, were belligerent and insisted that recipients go through the lengthy appeals process before they would waive the supposed debt. Rob couldn't help wondering how many people were simply accepting these debts and paying them all over the country without seeking advice first.

Then in the midst of this the new Treasurer, not known for his economic ability, decided to raise the spectre of a GST again. It became clear that the next election would be fought on this issue.

As the election approached, Rob and his team did everything they could to highlight to the Government and to voters that they agreed that the system needed reform, but that there was a lot within the current tax system that could be done, which would not require moving to an entirely new system. However, the Government wasn't listening. The Labor Party had convinced themselves that they could beat the Government on this issue, but they were to be disappointed. Out of the blue, the Democrats chose to start negotiating with the Government on a possible GST. Rob and his team were horrified; at no point had they expected the Democrats to consider the possibility of a goods and services tax. Immediately it became clear that if Labor lost the election a GST would be the result, as the Democrats could not be counted on to block it in the Senate.

The election became more than simply Rob's first as Leader of the Opposition. The Labor Party knew that low income and disadvantaged people would be worse off under a goods and services tax, and that it would be impossible to reverse once introduced. Rob and his colleagues knew that there had been much discussion in other countries which had previously introduced such taxes about the difficulty in getting rid of it once in place. This election was, in Rob's eyes, a battle for the economic future of low earners and disadvantaged people. He knew that the chances of dislodging a Government that had only been in place for one term were very low. Traditionally, Australian voters seemed to give Governments at least two terms to carry out their legislative programme.

Still they persisted, and when the Gooring Government was returned in 1998 Rob and his team were devastated. The sense of failure was palpable, and it was not alleviated when the Government succeeded in getting a bastardised form of their proposed GST through Parliament.

Rob's disappointment at losing such a fundamental battle was softened somewhat when Maggie finalised her first children's book and it was published. Jamie's publishing company, through whom Maggie had decided to go, had found a fabulous local artist to do the illustrations of the delightful characters and places Maggie had created for her book. To celebrate, Jamie and Paul had a small party at their lovely home and Rob made a point of being able to attend. The kids went to stay with his parents for the evening.

The dinner party started at 8 p.m., and when Maggie and Rob got there they realised they were the last to arrive. Maggie was thrilled to see her old lecturer, Jim, there with his partner, Moira. She greeted him like an old friend, aware that she would not possibly be in the position she was without him. She was really pleased to discover that Moira was every bit as lovely as her husband.

The other guests were an artist, Maeve, Jamie's brother, Karl, and their next door neighbour, Joel. Joel had a music shop in Fremantle specialising in old records. Rob was fascinated by this strange group of people. More interesting to him was the realisation that he was there solely because he was Maggie's husband. She was clearly the star of the show and he was merely a reasonably pleasant addition. Rob was used to people hightailing it over to him and grilling him on his policies and giving him unwanted advice about how to handle certain issues. Here he was largely left to his own devices, and had to consciously make an effort to be included. It wasn't that they were rude or unpleasant, simply that they were entirely uninterested in what he did. After an hour or so of discussions about art, records and how clever his wife was, he started to realise that he really enjoyed being Rob Connor for the evening, rather than the Leader of the Opposition.

He spoke at great length to Joel, a tall, lanky fellow with a fabulous mane of long, black hair. As Joel spoke with passion about his enormous collection of records, Rob was reminded that he had loved music at one point. He and Joel discussed his record collection, which he remembered was still at home in his parent's place. Joel got quite enthused about some of Rob's old Rolling Stones and Bob Dylan records. Rob found himself promising to bring them down to Joel's shop one Saturday morning.

Maeve was a completely neurotic artist, who had him in stitches telling him what she went through before each of her gallery showings. The agony of deciding what pieces to display a mere ten or twelve hours before it was due to open. She explained how she had to get her closest friends together who would strategically get her drunk enough to sleep heavily and then fill her up with Berocca and black coffee just before the big event. She giggled as she said that she was glad for the sake of her liver that she only had four or five big shows a year. Rob was totally fascinated by her.

Halfway through the evening he looked to find his wife laughing with no inhibitions at something that Karl and Jamie had said to her. She was totally at ease here and these people were clearly very good friends. He felt very relaxed himself, and he wasn't sure that it was entirely due to the fabulous Spanish red he had consumed in large quantities. These people didn't expect him to be the Leader of the Opposition, they were not sizing him up to see whether he would make a good PM. They were prepared to let him into their group to determine whether they liked Rob Connor the person. Their lives were filled with fun and beauty, they were not weighed down with the responsibility of running the world or feeling like they should. That's not to say they didn't feel that some of these issues were important; it was simply that they expressed themselves through their chosen art and moved on. He envied them. In this brief moment of complete clarity he envied them for knowing exactly who they were.

When he left, he felt that he had for the first time enjoyed adult company that stimulated him and yet required nothing of him but to be himself.

Maggie's book was launched the following day and she was asked to do a few book readings in local bookstores. The book was a success and within a few months was being posted on best-seller lists around the country. Maggie, who had spent the last few months on tenterhooks, was relieved more than excited about her book's success. It was certainly enough to get her focused on her next project, though, and many a night Rob found her madly typing away on her laptop.

Meanwhile, life in Parliament was very difficult. There was increasing pressure on Rob to pursue a harder line against the Government. He had even taken criticism that he was not tough enough. However, all criticism aside, his numbers were up and by 2001 he was leading Gooring in the polls. The voters obviously appreciated his distaste for simply opposing everything the Government did. By June 2001 he was clearly set to win the next election. He didn't let it remove his focus, though; whoever coined the phrase 'A week is a long time in politics' really knew what they were talking about.

By September 2001 the tide had well and truly turned. The eleventh day of September saw the ghastly scenes at the World Trade Center and the Pentagon. Rob had been in London and was due to fly out when news came. He saw Tony Blair speaking at a union conference, clearly emotional about the magnitude of the attacks on the US. The centre of London saw a change of pace almost immediately. This was a city used to protecting itself against terrorist attacks. He knew that international intelligence suggested that London was a very strong target.

He would never forget sitting in his hotel room, channel-flicking, waiting for his car to arrive to take him to Heathrow. He saw that *Diagnosis Murder* with Dick Van Dyke was due on in a few minutes, and he was a sucker for those '70s and '80s murder mystery shows. He flicked to BBC to watch it and was stunned by what greeted him. The sight appeared to be an explosion in what was clearly one of the World Trade Center towers. Gary raced through his door, ashen-faced with shock. They watched with horror as a plane crashed into the second tower.

'No way,' gasped Gary. 'No bloody way!'

They watched, horrified, now realising that this was in fact a terrorist attack they were witnessing. It couldn't be a movie, because no one would believe it. Within minutes Steve had joined them, his usually calm face registering shock and grief. They watched the ghastly scene unfold, the crash at the Pentagon and the collapse of the two towers. They were too horrified for tears as they saw people jumping out of the Trade Center windows to their deaths. The three men would always regret having seen these scenes as they happened, knowing that these people were actually dying as they watched.

A message came to tell them that Heathrow had been closed, as London expected a terrorist attack. They sat in silence for several minutes. Gary then leapt to his feet and ordered three very large brandies to be delivered to his room. He ensured that there were rooms for them all that night at the hotel. That was to prove inspired, as the next few hours would see travellers all over the city desperately looking for accommodation, as many had expected to fly home that day. London's airports were closed immediately so nobody would be leaving.

Steve and Rob drafted a message of sympathy to the US President and a press release. Rob then suggested that each of them retire to their rooms to ring their families. Rob and Maggie sat on opposite sides of the world and cried quietly into their handsets, desperately wishing they were together for this dreadful day. Rob spoke to the kids, who were confused and upset by the scenes they had witnessed. Not for the first time Rob rued the ability of the press to respond so quickly to a drama and record it for the world to witness. Although he recognised the value of these recordings, not least for historical purposes, the trauma they would cause worldwide would be massive. His children would not forget those scenes for many years.

It was into action after that. He was shocked to discover that Peter Gooring was in New York that day, thanks to a last minute change of plan. He tracked him down and had a quick word with him, ensuring that he and his team were okay. Gooring sounded old as he told him that the Australian Embassy in New York had confirmed that there were several hundred Australians working in the two towers that day. Most had not yet been accounted for.

Rob also made contact with No. 10 and let them know he was in London in case he could be of any use. He confirmed the whereabouts of Gooring for them, knowing that the US would be keen to retaliate quickly as a show of force.

Most of all he was keen to get back to Australia, who was without her PM or her Opposition Leader. Australians were in a panic over the possibility of attacks there. Rob knew that Australian cities were unlikely to be high on the list of international targets but he understood their fear anyway.

The next few days allowed him to see the stoicism of the British people. They just got up and went to work every day, in the midst of a plethora of bomb and other security scares. Security was upgraded in all Government buildings, and armed police and army vehicles roamed the streets in central London. But these people just got up and went to work, finding time in their days to provide immense support to their American cousins, many of whom were without places to stay and without their families in a time of grief. His regard for these people deepened in those few unexpected days in London.

In an effort to assist the isolated US citizens, Rob had organised for his staff to move into his larger room and remained paying for the other rooms so that the hotel could make them available to US citizens. The hotel, part of an American chain, was very grateful.

Finally they were able to fly out of Heathrow, leaving the hotel early to go through intensive security checks. They were bemused to discover that their food and drinks, within the airport, were served with plastic knives and forks. They arrived in Perth more than thirty hours after leaving the hotel and were shattered. Maggie had met Rob at the airport, with his driver, and looked more than a little relieved to see him home safe and sound. They dropped Steve at his home on the way; Gary had resolutely chosen to do the last leg home to Canberra that evening so he stayed at the airport.

Rob flew to Canberra two days later, noting the increased security and tension both in Perth and in the capital. Gooring was back, and the brief moment of camaraderie was gone. Perhaps that was because an election was on the way, and maybe it was selfish even to think it, but Rob knew that just a few short days ago he would have had to be hit by a bus not to win the next election. Now he was not so sure. Gooring had the entire country in a spin. People were genuinely terrified of a terrorist attack in Australia and although Rob knew that it was a possibility, the probability was not high. Osama Bin Laden and his network had other, much higher profile fish to fry, so to speak. He objected to what he saw as deliberately raising the fear levels of Australians for political gain. Part of it was reasonable, he knew, to ensure that people were more vigilant. It was impossible to totally protect people one hundred per cent of the time; the only possible way to avoid a terrorist attack was for people to stay aware. However, he objected to Gooring leading people to believe that an attack was imminent. He saw a huge difference in the way people reacted in Australia to the way they had behaved in Britain.

He also knew that if Australian people were afraid they would vote to keep Gooring in Government. Gooring's smug behaviour was hard to take. While he was shattered by what had happened in the US, he knew that it had saved his Prime Ministership. He called the election, and although Rob and his team battled hard, Gooring was elected PM again.

And that, thought Rob as he stood outside the Pemberton Street cottage, was exactly how he had ended up here. His dream lost, a backbencher now, with no hope of ever becoming Prime Minister. Finally he walked through the front door into the arms of his waiting wife.

Chapter Seven

Rob woke late the next morning after a night of disturbed sleep. His family were up already and trying to be very quiet in an attempt to not to wake him.

He rolled out of bed, washed his face and wandered downstairs to see them all. They looked up, clearly unsure how to react to him.

'Coffee, honey?' Maggie asked in a huge attempt to be cheerful.

'Sure – and what about we make up some pancakes? I got no place to be,' he replied with a little chuckle.

They all knew he was pretending to be upbeat, but laughed along with him anyway. After breakfast, Jack took Samantha out to get the Sunday papers from the deli so their parents could talk.

'How are you really, Rob?' Maggie asked, concern clearly evident in her voice.

'I really don't know. I guess I am numb – just waiting for it all to hit me,' he replied sombrely. 'I know this is going to hurt like hell but I feel like right now I am in denial.'

As if to torture him, the front pages of the newspapers the kids arrived back with were all splashed with headlines about Gooring's win and Rob's decision to stand down as leader. He would remain leader until a caucus meeting next week where his successor would be chosen. The phone calls would start soon from the factions seeking his support for their man or woman, as the case might be. In fact he was surprised that they hadn't already called, the faction numbers men (and they really were all men) weren't known for their sensitivity.

He was torn. He didn't want to stay at home to take the phone calls, but he didn't want to go out and put himself through the inevitable questions from the press and public either. Suddenly he stood up and said, 'Right, let's go and get some DVDs and popcorn and have a movie day.'

The kids – he would really have to stop calling them that now that Jack was practically a man – jumped up, cheering in agreement with his idea. He felt a pang in his chest that they were all at home with him on a weekend day when he felt sure they all had more interesting things to do.

The Connor family stepped out to the video shop and came back laden with DVDs and other essentials – popcorn and ice cream amongst them. Rob carefully unplugged the phone and walked back downstairs to where his family were waiting.

They had a lovely day, and he couldn't have imagined anything else he would rather have done, but as the day progressed and he grew more tired, he started to feel reality set in. There was a pain in his chest and he was surprised that an emotional hurt could actually be felt so physically. As the last movie finished he stood up and stretched saying, 'Wow, I am so tired, I think I will pop upstairs and have a sleep.'

Upstairs the grief overwhelmed him and he sat in his small bathroom and sobbed like he hadn't done for years and years. He felt the pain intensely now and realised that he was grieving for the loss of his dream. He had worked towards his goal for so long now, since he was five years old, and he just didn't know what he was going to do with himself. With his eyes red, both from crying and extreme tiredness, he came out of the bathroom and was almost grateful that sleep finally took away the gnawing in his gut.

When he woke up it was dark and Jack and Samantha had gone to bed. Maggie made him a sandwich and then forced him to have a brandy for 'medicinal purposes'. She had put the phone back on the hook and there were several messages. His parents and Maggie's had rung, and there were the expected dozen or so from Party people. He was touched to see that Jamie and Paul had rung.

'I didn't think that they did politics,' he commented to Maggie after hearing their message.

'They don't,' she said, 'but they are friends and they both know what it is like to lose something you want badly.'

He started to cry again and was embarrassed by himself. Maggie took him in her arms and said, 'I think you have to face facts, my darling, this is going to happen to you for a little while. Let it go, otherwise it will come out at the most inopportune moments.'

They both laughed at the thought of him breaking down in caucus or in Parliament. Soon they were imagining him breaking down during parliamentary debates about the expenditure figures on wheat bins, the price of petrol and \t other such ridiculous times. Goodness knows what made them think of it, but it did the trick and soon they were smiling again. Maggie gave him another brandy and sent him off to speak to his parents.

They were very sympathetic, and in true parental fashion told him how proud they were of him and that he would make a success of whatever he chose to do next. They also reminded him that Gooring had come from the backbench to become Prime Minister, against all the odds. He was incredibly surprised that they knew about Gooring, and not for the first time he was grateful to have John and Mary Connor as his parents.

The next few days were quite odd, much slower than the pace he had been required to work at for many, many years. He met with his advisors, aware that they too were going to have to find new jobs. However, he had warned them in advance of his intention to stand down as leader if he lost the election, and his commitment to ensuring that they found suitable employment. They briefed him on the press reaction to his retirement to the backbench. The press had been uncharacteristically generous. To be fair, he was aware that he and his party were not the only ones who had wanted to see the back of Gooring. Gary and Steve showed him a couple of the key editorials, which were surprisingly complimentary. Just like an obituary, he thought wryly.

After discussing the caucus meeting later in the week and the lead contenders, Steve went to check his messages. Gary told him that he had been offered several positions. One – he laughed – was with one of Australia's leading media magnates, and the second was as a Director of Public Affairs within the entertainment industry. He clearly intended to have further discussions about the latter. Rob wished him the best of luck, and told him that he would support him in any way that might be helpful. He also considered that they should get together with all of the staff for a send-off of sorts. Rob had already spoken to the Deputy Premier in Western Australia, Ian, who had gladly offered Steve the Chief of Staff position in his office. Steve was very pleased with this offer; he had worked with Ian previously and the two men got on together very well. Although he didn't say it, Rob knew that, like himself, Steve found it hard to be away from his wife and children so often, and his new position would provide him with extra time with them.

The caucus meeting seemed to come up more quickly than Rob expected. He had been advised, and had reached the same conclusion independently himself, to support his deputy, Tom, for the position of leader. Tom was a good man, who had strong convictions and would stick to them. There were those in the party who did not consider that he would come across well on the media, but Rob didn't think that should be the deciding factor. After a comparatively event-free caucus meeting, Tom was confirmed as leader. As Rob walked from the caucus room he was confronted by the throng of waiting media questioning him about how he felt about Tom replacing him. Rob was effusive in his praise. He had no reason not to be; Tom would be a good and ethical leader.

He flew immediately back to Perth with Steve, glad for once for the Prime Minister's timing of the election, which meant that the Parliament would not sit again until after the Christmas break. He would go home and have some time out with his family, maybe even go on a holiday.

He arrived home to a family determined not to let him fall into a slump. Maggie and the kids dragged him off to all sorts of events and on all sorts of wild goose chases. One night as he was sitting on the lounge curled up with a mystery novel, which he was really gripped by, Maggie flew through the door and said, 'Get up now and make sure that you can find your thermals.'

He looked up from his book, the expression on his face suggesting that anyone who would be looking for their thermals in 37° heat must be a few cents short of a dollar.

'Come on!' she urged excitedly. 'We're going on a holiday and you are going to love it.'

'What do you mean we're going on holiday? It's nearly Christmas, and where could we be going that we would need thermals?' Rob asked, somewhat bemused. Reluctantly he put down his book and followed her upstairs.

Maggie was frantically pulling out suitcases as he

reached the top of the stairs. Excitement was causing two bright spots to stand out on her cheeks. Rob stood and watched her for a few moments and then took her hand and sat her down on the bed.

'Now slowly, what is happening here *exactly*?' he asked deliberately.

Maggie, words tumbling over each other, told him that she had booked them to go to Russia for a holiday. They would be spending Christmas in Red Square.

'But we need visas, and that takes ages,' he said.

'Ah, but I'm not just a pretty face,' she retorted laughing. 'I rang Steve, he got on to the Embassy and they will have the visas delivered here tomorrow. The fact that both of us have been security cleared at such a high level has apparently helped the process. I have tickets, new jackets and the kids will stay with Mum and Dad. They'll go to your mum and dad's for Christmas dinner.'

Rob sat back and breathed deeply. He had always wanted to go to Russia, fascinated by its innate beauty and its long and proud history. He had forgotten until that very moment how much he had loved history, with a particular interest in Eastern Europe; he supposed it was just because it was so very different to what he had grown up with.

'I can't believe it,' Rob declared. 'What about your book?'

She laughed. 'Jamie has given me time off for good behaviour.'

Rob helped pack in a daze, he still couldn't believe

that he was going to Russia. Maggie had done this, gifting him a lifetime experience to help get him out of the doldrums. Yet again, for the thousandth time, he thanked God for his beautiful wife...

The next few days ran by in a blur. He had no time to think about how devastated he was by the election result. Maggie seemed to have received an extra dose of adrenalin from somewhere. Three days after her announcement they were winging their way towards London where they would spend two days with friends in the city, and then they would be on their way to Moscow. The only downsides were the significant increase in security, resulting in them having to arrive more than three hours before their flight, and the length of the flight. Rob had never been a fan of long haul flights, and this one was no exception. Maggie had really splashed out and managed to get two very decently priced first class seats. Rob had never flown first class before and was set to enjoy it. The service was exceptional and the food was the best he'd ever eaten on an airline.

Rob took the very rare opportunity to lose himself in his novel and to watch several movies without the phone and its inevitable interruptions. He read and slept for hours, waking only to consume more coffee and delectable food. He made it a policy not to drink alcohol on long flights because he found he was dehydrated enough without adding alcohol to the mix. Unfortunately he was not as self-disciplined about his caffeine intake.

Maggie kept herself busy. She had brought her laptop along and was happily creating magic for young children. Rob wondered how she could feel inspired to write wherever she was. After a few hours she stretched her arms and packed up her work. They sat companionably watching a romantic movie together. Afterwards they fell asleep for a few hours, with Maggie leaning her sweet-smelling head on his shoulder.

They had had a brief stop in Singapore, where it was extremely hot and humid, even inside the airport. After a longer sleep and being woken up to hot rolls and coffee, they read for a while longer. Rob was starting to get edgy after about eighteen hours in the air. He had enjoyed the prospect of doing nothing for a few hours, but this was too much. He thought ruefully that if they would only open the door now, he really would get off!

They arrived at Heathrow and were immediately thrown into a huge security operation. It was well over an hour and a half before they had their suitacses and were heading towards the taxi rank. They had momentarily considered the Heathrow Express, but they were just too tired to negotiate it with all their luggage. They were relieved to see that there were not too many people queuing in front of them. Within fifteen minutes they were on their way to their friends, Kerry and Tony, in Pimlico. Maggie fell asleep within three minutes of settling in the black cab.

They arrived at the small stucco fronted terrace

house in St George's Drive within thirty-five minutes, and a surprisingly bright and cheery couple greeted them at the front door. Tony already had fresh coffee brewing and the two of them laughed at the memory of the dreadful coffee they had had to endure in their first visit to London more than twenty years before. The Drews popped the Connors bags in their room and the four caught up on all of the news over the past few months. Unlike other friends and family, the Drews were not awkward over the subject of his election defeat and subsequent stepping down. Tony and Kerry ragged him mercilessly about letting such a short bloke beat him again! They were all laughing within minutes, and Rob realised that he had needed them not to pity him; he'd had his fill of sympathy over the last month.

Within a couple of hours Maggie and Rob had thrown all of the prevailing theory to the wind and gone to bed. They slept heavily in the beautiful, cosy bedroom for nearly four hours. They woke up and showered, and went downstairs to see their hosts. That night they all walked down to The Contented Vine, a fabulous wine bar and restaurant just a few minutes walk from the Drews' place. The food was spectacular. Their risotto, which hadn't been on the menu in September when Rob was last there, was fantastic. They chatted for hours over three courses and many bottles of red wine – Australian, in fact.

When they had finished, they strolled down to the Thames with their coats wrapped tight around them, walking over to the south side of Vauxhall Bridge and towards the new MI6 building with its rather odd green windows. Rob stood there with the others and looked over the sight that never ceased to take his breath away. The Palace of Westminster, even on this drizzly, grey winter evening in London, was stunning. It stood proud and tall against the darkening sky, the mother of all Parliaments. He stood as if in awe for five minutes or so and then turned to leave with the others. Nobody witnessing the scene would have believed that he had seen that very same view too many times to count.

The next day was a real London stunner. He was always amazed that the city could do sunny days without the heat. It was a mild 10° but they took gloves and scarves with them, knowing that London, unlike Perth, could get significantly colder in the middle of the day.

They walked down for a late breakfast at Caramel in Wilton Road and were reminded how much they loved their routine when they visited this fantastic city. After a leisurely couple of hours reading the newspapers, they walked down through St James's Park and onto Oxford Street, buying gifts for the kids. Jack had pre-ordered a Beckham football shirt, and they did not have to walk far before they had more choices than they could possibly count.

All too soon their couple of days in London were up and they boarded a plane to Moscow with all the eager anticipation of first-time travellers. The flight was a mere four hours, although neither were happy to be back on a plane so soon after their twenty-two-hour journey to London. Before they knew it they were at Domodedovo Airport. They had booked themselves into the National Hotel, a five star hotel in the centre of Moscow city. The traffic was unbelievable; only in Bangkok had they seen traffic the likes of this. The taxi trip into the centre took one and a half hours, and it seemed that drivers did not feel in any way restricted by the limits of the traffic lanes painted along the highway.

Despite the poverty evident everywhere, Rob was overwhelmed by the fact that he was finally here. The driver had a CD of Russian music playing in the hotel taxi and Rob, although he had no idea what they were singing about, loved it.

When they finally arrived at the hotel they were impressed by the service that they received. The Russian staff were efficient and registered them very quickly, despite the added visa registration requirements. Rob really appreciated that their efficient service was not the fake, cloying familiarity evident in other parts of the world. They were shown to their lovely room, and when they looked out of the window they had their first glimpse of the city they had come to see. The city was covered in a light snow and the Kremlin glittered in the moonlight.

Unable to resist, they grabbed their coats, scarves and hats and went out into the Moscow night, remembering to take copies of their passport and visas, their mobile and embassy number. They had been warned that since the advent of capitalism the police supplemented their seriously inadequate wages by 'finding' problems with tourist visas, requiring bribes to resolve. It took no time at all to find Red Square, and Rob found himself standing in the middle of the place that he had dreamed all of his life of coming to. In that moment as he took in the eastern beauty of this magnificent city, he realised that some dreams unexpectedly do come true.

Maggie was smitten. 'Who knew that this place was so incredible?'

They turned and the grandeur of St Basil's Cathedral rose before them. Photos did not do this building justice, it was fantastic, unlike anything they had ever seen. It was closed, so they couldn't go in and instead stood for a few moments in front of the Mausoleum in which Lenin's body was displayed. Rob had read a funny story about when Stalin was buried with Lenin in the Mausoleum. An old Bolshevik madam had a dream that Lenin was very unhappy about being stuck with his successor, and as a result Stalin was moved out and buried behind the Mausoleum. He laughed as he remembered the story, although he was fairly sure that he wouldn't have been happy stuck with Stalin indefinitely, either. Maggie gave him an odd look but didn't ask, so he didn't explain.

They wandered back toward the hotel, as it was extremely cold, and ordered some very Russian delicacies to celebrate their first night there. Caviar, blinis and vodka were brought up and, because they had been told it was the best in the world, Russian ice cream. They enjoyed their feast, sitting at the small table in the room, overlooking the Kremlin.

The next day they rose late and ordered some coffee and breakfast. The coffee was excellent and woke them up. When they got downstairs they had a chat with Svetlana, who helped them organise some tours. She had them organised within twenty short minutes and they were off. As they had a few hours until their Kremlin tour started, Svetlana gave them a map and let them know where they needed to meet the tour leader. They wandered through Voskresenskiye Vorota – Resurrection Gate to the uninitiated – and back to the impressive cobbled square. They were just in time to go in and see Lenin's body in the Mausoleum. They joined the rather lengthy line and made their way through the small building. Rob found himself rather moved to see Lenin lying there, even though he did look remarkably like a waxwork. How impressive of the Russians to preserve Lenin's body for public view, especially given that he had died in 1924.

The day flew by for them as they wandered the streets of Moscow, going into the Kremlin, which was startlingly beautiful. They particularly liked the small rooms at the top of the building where the Tsars had met with visiting statesmen and women. These apartments were smaller, as in early years they had been hard to keep warm. Rob could picture them all sitting in the tiny, rounded rooms. There was a scattering of artists sketching the rooms all around the Kremlin, yet another reminder of the Russian's love of art.

The next day was Christmas Day back home in Oz, but not for the Russians, who celebrate Christmas on 7 January. Rob and Maggie met some English travellers on the City Tour – which they had finally found the meeting place for after matching the Cyrillic address with those on the map. Susan was a teacher on a short holiday and Terry was living in Japan and on his way home to see his family. They thoroughly enjoyed the tour and in particular the view from Universitetskaya Ploschad, near Moscow University, over Moscow. They bought fabulous trinkets at the markets there and took photos of the landscape before them.

Christmas lunch was one they would never forget, all-you-can-eat pizza at Gum Department Store This was a Christmas Day that would go down as a first for them.

A few days later they left for St Petersburg. The airport itself was an experience. It was tiny and nothing like anything they had seen before. It was fairly basic and bustling with people; it felt like a very eastern experience, and then, just to totally confuse their categorisation, Dido's dulcet tones came at them from out of the airport speakers. Rob and Maggie looked at each other and laughed. Fortunately the check-in staff's English was markedly better than their attempts at Russian and they were finally on their way.

The flight was short and sweet, and they arrived at St

Petersburg to find that the hotel had arranged a driver to meet them at the airport. The drive in was short and they were surprised to discover that St Petersburg was much more European in style than Moscow. Their hotel was the incredibly lovely Corinthia Palace in Nevsky Prospekt, the main street in St Petersburg. While Rob checked in Maggie managed to organise a private car for them with their very own tour guide to take them around the city the following day. What absolute luxury! They woke early and met Katya, their tour guide, downstairs in the lobby. Katya was fantastic, she knew everything about her home city and its history. Sergei, their driver, was pleasant and very helpful; he regularly stopped in great spots for them to get out and walk and take photos. It really was the most pleasant tour they had ever been on.

They were amazed by the St Peter and Paul Cathedral. It was a beautiful edifice containing the coffins of Russia's royalty. It was an odd set-up, really, with the coffins just laid out all over the floor. The Tsar and his wife, who had been responsible for abolishing slavery, were housed in stunningly beautiful coffins, painstakingly carved out of marble. The big surprise was finding where Princess Anastasia was buried. Maggie and Rob exchanged bemused looks and asked Katya why it was that they had been subjected to millions, give or take a few, of documentaries, movies and books on the subject of the location of Anastasia Romanova, who reportedly escaped those who killed her family.

Katya shrugged. 'I don't know, many people say the same thing. The remains that were not found were those of the heir, Alexei, but there were traces of acid found with the bodies, so it has been assumed that the acid destroyed his remains.'

Maggie and Rob were yet again reminded of how much garbage they were fed through some of the media. They had thought it was a fact that Anastasia had been able to escape.

Peter the Great's grave was also there, and this caused them a moment of reflection. They had known very little about him until they had arrived in Russia, yet he had obviously been a compelling character. The little they did know about him suggested that he would have been much better suited to being an explorer than a Tsar.

They went shopping at one of St Petersburg's many tourist shops and bought a collection of scarves, paintings of the city's beautiful sights, small babushkas and many other wonderful souvenirs, which they would regret having bought when they had to traipse it all back to the other side of the world.

Next, it was back to the hotel, and on the way Rob quizzed Katya about the changeover to capitalism and asked her how it had affected her family and friends. Katya did not commit herself to saying whether she supported communism or capitalism but did say that under the old system people always had food, clothing, employment and even family holidays in the Crimea. They had not had much choice, but people knew they could afford to live. She said that her parents could no longer afford to live in their small flat, and her children, though earning meagre wages themselves had to help out to make ends meet. Culturally, Russian parents tended to help their children, and it had been very difficult for her parents to have this situation reversed. She stated that there certainly were more choices but that very few had the money to take them up. The cost of things had risen hugely since the changeover, and many were afraid of where they would end up, particularly older people. Katya added that one thing that saddened her was that Russian people had always been able to visit art galleries, theatres and museums whenever they had wanted to and now, despite the significant discounts for Russian citizens, not all could afford to go.

Rob found this very sad and was reminded that as a young person he had admired the principles of communism; it was how it operated in practice that concerned him. Katya and Sergei had said that ordinary people did not feel afraid under communism, they went about their business without fear or pressure, whatever western propaganda said about this. Despite this, Rob knew that there had been significant levels of control and pressure on those who had expressed their opposition to the Russian communist state, and wondered whether it would be possible for a communist government to operate without the extraordinary level of control that it seemed to require to function. He had had this discussion with a friend who had left China just prior to the Tiananmen Square protests, who indicated that communism was a great ideal, but humans were basically too selfish to live for long in such a system.

Rob and Maggie left Russia a few days later and felt buoyed by their experience there. They had really liked the Russians, who appeared to them to be very proud and friendly, yet without the overly familiar attitude towards tourists found elsewhere. Tourists would be looked after in the same way as anyone else, but Russian people didn't seem overly concerned that tourists visit.

The flight home was uneventful, but long. They arrived back in Perth and they headed home to get a good night's sleep before they picked the kids up the next day. It had only been two and a half weeks, but Rob felt like something significant had shifted for him. He had been reminded that once it had been overwhelmingly important to him to protect low income and disadvantaged people, yet he had had to go to another country to see that some had many choices in life and some barely had enough to get by in their very basic lifestyle. He had once wanted to change the balance and redistribute wealth and opportunities to the less well off. He had tried, but somehow he had lost sight of how important this was to him.

Well, I have heaps of time on my hands to rethink my position on this now, he thought wryly.

Chapter Eight

The months following his return went slowly for Rob, despite the elaborate distraction his wife had provided for him over Christmas. Gradually, all of his staffers found jobs except for his electorate staff, whom he was able to keep on.

Soon he was unable to distract himself from the significant change to his role. The sense of desolation and isolation was intense. In Canberra, his Shadow Cabinet colleagues were debating international strife, defence, employment, education and other such critical issues. Yet here he was sitting in his electorate office far from everything politically he deemed really important. He had not gone to Canberra so often since he had stood down as leader. He found it very, very difficult to sit on the backbenches and avoid strongly rebutting the tenuous and unsubstantiated arguments coming from Gooring and his equally ineffectual cronies.

To fill the time he had increased his appointments with his constituents and local community groups. He had not had much time to meet with them as a Minister and as the Leader of the Opposition.

However, he thought sadly, this isn't going to fill the gaping hole that losing my lifetime dream has left...

His electorate staff, who had previously dealt with

most constituent and community group enquiries, now set up meetings with those they felt would benefit from his personal intervention.

One of the first people through his door was a quiet man from El Salvador and his interpreter. Jesus was applying for a Disability Support Pension because of the injuries he had suffered after being shot. Rob was horrified and then had to laugh when Jesus grinned widely and said that it didn't get him out of housework! However, the talk turned serious when Rob took the opportunity to ask Jesus about the war in El Salvador. Jesus' face clouded as he recounted the devastation and terror of his country's civil war. Suddenly he looked Rob directly in the eye and told him something, and the interpreter swallowed hard as he translated,

'Jesus says that he could handle it when he saw his friends die in front of him but he truly couldn't handle seeing his children shot dead in front of him.'

Jesus was crying quietly now, and Rob's eyes filled with tears as he leant across the desk and took the man's hand in his own.

'I am so sorry, I am just so sorry,' he said, his voice choking with emotion.

He turned to see that the interpreter himself had given way to tears and they slid unchecked down his cheeks. He wondered how often interpreters would hear such horrific stories.

Rob got up and walked to his office door and asked if someone would mind getting him and his guests coffee, tea and biscuits. He then moved them all to the small couch and armchairs in the corner of his office. They talked quietly and drank the sweetened tea that had been brought in for them. Suddenly Rob realised that he may be no expert but this man in front of him was clearly suffering post-traumatic stress disorder and really needed his help with Centrelink to negotiate for him.

But can I broach the subject with this man? he wondered. I know nothing about the cultural norms in El Salvador for dealing with mental and emotional issues. Then he realised that Jesus had been straight with him throughout this entire meeting and he owed it to him to treat him with the same respect.

'Jesus,' he started, 'do you think that there any chance you could be suffering post-traumatic stress disorder?' He waited for the interpreter to ask the question, fearful that Jesus would be upset by it.

To his relief, Jesus nodded and spoke to him through the interpreter. 'Yes, I don't know what it is called, but I cry often and I cannot stop thinking of these things. I cannot sleep and I am always jumping when I hear any loud noises. I wake up yelling sometimes from nightmares and sweating very much. I do not think I am a weak man but I cannot stop my feelings about this.'

After this answer Rob felt sure that he was on the right track. After asking Jesus to sign a document giving him permission to speak to Centrelink on his behalf, Rob walked through to a smaller office and rang the local branch. He had not always found Centrelink staff to be overly helpful but his people had assured him that the local Wilson office staff were very cooperative. He spoke to Jenny, a bright and bubbly lady, who was distinctly unimpressed about speaking to him, obviously thinking he was only calling her to score political points. However, he was gratified to discover that her attitude changed once she heard what he had to say. She clearly knew Jesus well and said in amazement, 'I have been trying to put my finger on what it is that is going on with Jesus, and to think that you managed it in only a few minutes! I think you are absolutely right. Would you tell him from me that I am going to get him an appointment with the Department Psychologist for an initial assessment, and he will receive a letter confirming all of this within the next two days. I can't guarantee it 100%, but I am fairly sure that this will secure his Disability Support Pension, and he shouldn't have to worry too much about reviews, either – we have no interest in this office in forcing people back to work if they unable to do it.'

Rob was amazed by her efficiency. He knew that Centrelink really needed more staff to deal with their massive workload, yet here was someone so clearly eager to help. He walked through to his office and advised Jesus what had happened. The man was overwhelmed and shook Rob's hand for a long few minutes, with his good hand, thanking him profusely. Rob advised to come back immediately if he had any problems at all.

Jesus left the office obviously feeling that he could

rest a little easier. Rob realised it must be terrifying to think that you may have no income to pay the bills. He made a few notes and then handed the file back to his staff, letting them know that he wanted to be informed immediately if there was any further contact from Jesus. As he walked back to his office, he turned suddenly and asked, 'How many cases do we get like that one? How many people do we get with really serious issues similar to that?'

Eleanor replied, 'Most of them that we take on are at least that serious. We get the odd person who is delusional and suffering mental illness, and the occasional person who just wants to vent his or her spleen, but actually most people don't come to us until they really feel that they have nowhere else to go.'

Rob made a vague 'Hmm' sound and walked distractedly back to his office. In a few short minutes he felt that he had made a significant difference to Jesus' life. Here was a man who had had such an awful time, living through the tragedy of seeing his country torn apart by war and the devastation of seeing his children killed in front of him and not being able to do anything about it. Rob felt ashamed at thinking that this wasn't what was really important. It was so important to be able to touch people's lives, even in a minor way, and make them better. This was the coalface. What was making policy about, after all, if it wasn't to make people's lives better?

He saw some odd cases over the next few days, including a delightful indigenous woman, Dot, who had allegedly been overpaid by Centrelink and was about to start having her Centrelink payments cut to virtually nothing in order to pay it back. She was hilarious, maintaining her infectious sense of humour throughout their whole meeting, despite the fact that she was about to be living off very little money. Dot had a sick husband at home and needed to feed him special foods for his condition, yet didn't seem to be getting any special assistance for that. Rob wondered how she coped, even with her whole benefit. Finally they came down to the crux of the problem – a printing error showed that she had earned one million dollars in a particular fortnight! Rob roared with laughter as Dot said to him demurely, 'Look, fella, I don't do anything good enough to get that sort of money!' This absurd payslip appeared to be the cause of this whole situation, and Rob was annoyed that the matter had been allowed to get this far. He asked Dot if she had taken it in to show Centrelink and explained the mistake.

'Well, my mate down the deli copied it for me, and my bank thingo, and sent it to them, but they say they lost it and I don't like going into them Government places. My friend says that you people can fix stuff so I come here instead,' she replied.

Rob felt that it would be inappropriate for him to point out at that juncture that he was, in fact, government as well. Within a few short minutes Centrelink had grudgingly accepted the mistake and explained that Dot would receive a letter confirming that the debt had been overturned. After she left, showing very little surprise that Rob had been able to fix it, he asked one of his staff to research whether there was any help to pay for the special foods that her husband required, and to get back to him.

He realised as he wrote notes on Dot's file about the status of her case, that this job did indeed bring him into contact with some very interesting people, people who he had previously been unlikely to meet up with. Briefly he considered who the vast majority of his friends and colleagues were and realised with horror that they were a homogeneous bunch. They were largely all white middle-class people with qualifications. When had this happened to him? he wondered. Maggie's group of friends were much less predictable than his own, it seemed. It hadn't always been like this, he was sure.

Over the next few months Rob met with a huge range of people and local community groups. He had had no real idea of how many groups operated in his electorate and made it a point to find out. He asked his staff to organise drinks at the office and to invite as many groups as possible so he could get a better chance to meet some of the people involved. He started accepting as many invitations as possible to functions and Annual General Meetings, as long as they didn't conflict with his and Maggie's commitment to spend weekends together with the kids. He had been surprised to discover that his kids spent a lot of time at home on weekends now, something he'd reckoned to be the last thing that kids would want to do.

One Friday night, he walked through the door and Maggie smiled at him, saying, 'Hi love, would you like a glass of red?'

He nodded and sat his weary body down on the couch. She joined him a few minutes later carrying two glasses of the promised red wine. She looked at him and smiled warmly, and he picked up their glasses of wine and set them down on the table.

'What are you smiling at, Maggie mine?' he asked, taking her into his arms.

'I'm smiling at the obvious contentment on your face. You are tired but really happy at the moment,' she answered.

He thought about it for a minute, and yes, he really was happy with his life right now. He had really enjoyed connecting with his constituents and helping them work through some of the difficulties they faced on a day-to-day basis. He somehow felt as though he had learnt something significant over the past few months. He had always believed that he really understood his constituents and their wants and needs, but had not really noticed when he had started to take his eye off the ball. He couldn't recall when he started to lose sight of the reason for his passion to write good policy. He needed to take this time he now had to reconnect with people and find out what was happening in their lives.

'I really am,' he replied, surprised. 'I feel as though I am finding out what is important to me again.'

His wife smiled enigmatically and Rob wondered whether she had already known the answer before she asked the question.

Maggie had completed her second children's book and was very happy with it. Rob reflected how far she had come in confidence since her first meeting with Jamie. Her first book, while not a worldwide bestseller, had done really well, especially in Australia, where Australian kids could relate to the characters and the places described in the text. Jamie had managed to publish her book in the UK as well. Maggie had also been asked by some local primary schools to come and read parts of her story to children in grades one to three. She particularly loved that task. The second was being edited now and they expected to publish it later that year.

Jack was due to finish high school at the end of this year and neither of his parents could believe that he was so grown-up. He was doing particularly well this year, and had really come into his own. His study skills were impressive and his teachers had said that his work had improved in the past six months or so. Rob knew that this must have something to do with the fact that he had more time to invest in his son. Jack was a quiet, reflective and intelligent young man with a great sense of humour. Maggie and Rob felt relieved and proud that their son had not caused them anywhere near the grief that their friend's teenagers seem to have given them. One of Jack's best friends, Pete, to whom he remained intensely loyal, was regularly smoking marijuana, resulting in violent mood swings and serious antisocial behaviour. Rob and Maggie felt particularly sympathetic towards him as they both knew people who had practically lived on the stuff when they had been younger and they had never had this type of response. Neither of them had more than dabbled in it even when they were much younger, not liking the lack of control. Pete was still allowed over to their house to spend time with Jack, as neither parent wanted to isolate him, and they admired their son's loyalty.

And Samantha? Well, Samantha was a whole other question. They had a few repeats of the no homework behaviour but had reinstituted the dreaded grounding and no TV rule suggested by Ingrid, and after a few tantrums, their daughter had finally seen sense. However, no amount of cajoling could get her to turn in good work. She would rush through it and repeatedly hand in sub-standard work. They had all tried, even Jack, but Samantha wasn't buying into anything. Her teachers were tearing their hair out, frustrated that someone so capable of good work would simply not try. Rob and Maggie were both at a loss. Growing up they had each had clear goals, and these kept them working hard throughout their school and university life. Jack was similar to them in this. He was absolutely clear that he wanted to go to university and become a science teacher. Neither parent could quite understand where his ability in science came from, as both had all but flunked high school science units. However, this 'fad', as they had both initially thought it was, had lasted for two long years and they had come to realise that he would indeed be a science teacher.

It was Rob's father, John, who was to make the breakthrough. He had retired and retirement didn't really suit the old guy. Initially he had hung around the house so much that he had nearly driven Rob's mother crazy. Finally Mary Connor had insisted that he find himself a hobby or a new job, because no married couple should have to be together twenty-four hours a day, seven days a week!

John had skulked down to the rickety garage at the back of the yard and decided to clean it out through lack of anything else productive to do. He cleaned it out and found by accident several wood carvings and old woodwork pieces he had made near on twenty years before. He sat on an old box and found himself wondering why he had stopped making these trinkets and furniture, which he had really loved making so long ago. He could find no reasonable excuse, so in a moment of clarity he decided to clean out the garage, set himself up down there and make things. He had always loved the feeling of creating something with his own hands and watching it take shape before his very eyes.

For the next week Mary Connor almost regretted banishing her husband, as she hardly saw him. He cleared and cleaned, putting up shelves and throwing out rubbish that they had stored for years and never ever used. He bought himself tools and even got himself a small fridge for his beloved apple and pear juice.

Mary wandered down to the 'new' garage for a gander one day, and was surprised to see him happily setting himself up and humming to Roy Orbison as it played on the ancient cassette player on a small wooden bench. He was as content as she had ever seen him.

Four days later he presented her with a beautiful coffee table to replace the battered old one next to her arm chair. She was touched that his first creation should be something for her, and stunned at the beauty of it.

Rob, Maggie and the kids still often went down to his parents' place for Sunday lunch, and they were amazed at the change in John. Usually a quiet man, he was animated and keen to show them what he was working on. At first they didn't really take any notice, but Samantha disappeared as soon as she could get away to join her grandfather in his garage. He seemed quite happy to have her there watching him work. After a few weeks Samantha's parents noticed that whenever they were looking for her to leave that they always found her perched on a small wooden box, sombrely watching John. They were pleased that she was developing an even stronger relationship with her grandfather and thought nothing more of it… that is, until the impossible happened! Samantha proudly brought a B-plus home on her major maths assignment for the semester. Maggie and Rob were fortunately able to cover their astonishment quickly and praised her cleverness and hard work. As a special treat to celebrate they went out and got Samantha's choice of DVD for when dinner and homework was finished that night. As they were getting the car keys, Rob said to Maggie, 'Who has kidnapped our child and replaced her with this responsible little person?'

Maggie giggled and said, 'I don't know – maybe we should ask her what has happened.'

They agreed that they would not make too much of a fuss but, when they had a chance to bring it up, casually they would. As it happened Samantha provided the very opportunity they had been looking for. A few nights after revealing her impressive maths assignment mark Samantha climbed the stairs to her mother's study and asked her for help with her homework. Maggie avoided the impulse to swoon dramatically on her chair in shock, not wishing for her newly academic daughter to revert to type.

The problematic homework was an English assignment, a fact for which Maggie was pleased, as her knowledge of late primary school subjects was frankly a little faded. The assignment was to be a story of their choice about a holiday they had had. Samantha knew that she wanted to write about the holiday they had had at Karri Valley just outside Pemberton, but she didn't know how to write about it. From her own experience, Maggie knew that it was only getting started that was the problem; after you broke that particular barrier the rest just flowed. She suggested that they get a hot drink, and that Samantha sit down and tell her what she liked about the holiday and then they could work out what to write. Samantha thought that was a great idea and genuinely seemed grateful for her mum's help. While they were making hot, chocolatey Milo drinks, Maggie decided to ask the dreaded question.

'So, Sam,' she started, using her daughter's pet name, 'you have been getting some good marks. Why the sudden interest in your schoolwork?' She held her breath and waited for what could be a grumpy response. To her surprise the mystery was revealed.

'Grandy,' she said, referring to Rob's father, 'said that I can't go to college and do woodwork if I don't get good marks in school.' Maggie exhaled while her daughter continued, full of importance, as she imparted her newly gained knowledge to her mother. 'You can't measure up stuff without maths or write quotes and stuff without English, you know.'

Recovering quickly, Maggie asked, 'What sort of things do you want to make, my darling?'

'You know – tables and bookcases and stuff, like Grandy does,' her daughter replied.

'Wow! When did you decide this, Sam?'

'I have been helping Grandy in his shed and he makes the most beautiful things, like for Nanna,' Samantha answered.

Maggie had to agree and, even if this was a phase, she was going to do everything in her power to encourage it. It was the first sign of any sort of planning or ambition that they had seen from their daughter.

They sat down at the large wooden table in the dining room and began work on Samantha's assignment. As Maggie suspected, once Samantha started thinking about what it was she liked about her holiday she got enthusiastic and began frantically writing. Waiting for a few minutes to make sure she wasn't needed further, Maggie left and walked back up the stairs to resume her own work, thinking as she walked that she couldn't wait for Rob to get home so she could pass the news on to him.

She didn't have long to wait. Clearly the branch meeting he had been attending had finished early and at 9 p.m. she heard him come through the door. Samantha was still working on her assignment when Rob went through the dining room and up the stairs to change. He looked quizzically at Maggie and said quietly, 'It surely is not possible that I have just seen Samantha downstairs still working on her homework at nine o'clock at night…'

Maggie grinned and said, 'It is not only possible but highly probable – she came upstairs earlier to ask me for help.'

Rob fell on the bed dramatically feigning shock, his wife giggled. '*And*,' she continued, 'I have news. I know the answer to our little question.'

'No way!' he said breathless, 'You *are* good!'

Maggie relayed the story to him and he sat down with a thump on the bed. 'Wow – a cabinetmaker! That's what she is saying, isn't it?'

Maggie nodded, enjoying the fact that her husband was every bit as enthralled by the unveiling of their family mystery as she had been. They talked for a few minutes and discussed how they could encourage their daughter in her newly discovered ambition. Maggie suggested that he engage in some subterfuge and speak to his father to get some advice on this. He agreed with this proposition and said he would report back the following evening.

The following day Rob had a fairly easy run and so he decided to pop over to see his father. His parents were very surprised to see his car pull into the driveway. He realised that he hadn't done that since he was at uni. He had a cup of tea with them before bringing up the subject that had brought him to see them.

'A cabinetmaker!' his mother exclaimed.

'Yes, and apparently she got the idea from Grandy,' he said, turning his attention to his father.

'Well, she never actually used the word cabinetmaker to me,' his father replied quietly, 'but she is very interested in woodwork, and from what I have seen she is quite good at it as well. It's a pity that they don't offer it at her school.'

'What do you mean, "she's good at it?"' Rob asked, full of curiosity.

'A cabinetmaker!' his mother repeated in wonder.

They walked down to the garage, where Rob's father showed them the small table that he had been working on and proudly displayed the ornate leg that Samantha had helped with. He also indicated a couple of small figures and said that Samantha had done them by herself. One was obviously a dog, though the exact identity of the other creature wasn't entirely clear. Despite being a bit primitive, they unquestionably showed a natural talent. Rob was extremely proud of his daughter, thinking that such talent must obviously skip a generation. Then he remembered his exact task and asked his father how he could encourage this ambition.

His father, always a fount of advice, suggested a simple process of encouraging her, and if her interest started to develop further maybe they could purchase some beginner's materials to get her started. He reckoned that it would help if, while this interest was still in its early stages, Samantha spent time with people who shared her interest, including himself. Rob thought that this was sound advice. He thanked his parents, hugging them before returning to fill in his partner in crime on developments.

Chapter Nine

Life progressed quite normally, and Rob found himself heavily involved in several complex constituent cases. He had developed a new respect for his electorate staff, who had been dealing with these matters for years on his behalf. He still spent a great deal of time in Parliament but his sense of frustration was intense at now being relegated to the backbenches and being unable to contribute to the debate on issues that were really important to him; especially now that he felt that he had reconnected with his electorate and had a clearer idea of what issues were important to them in their lives.

Recently, he had become increasingly frustrated by the number of similar cases he had before him. He realised that the only way he could assist a great number of people at the same time was to influence policy. He already knew this and had known it for a long time, but all of a sudden he 'knew' it more than he had for years. He felt his commitment and motivation renewed.

He took his electorate staff out for lunch at a local Italian place and they talked about ways that they could use their time and resources to influence policy. His staff were thrilled that he had asked for advice on these issues, and not for the first time he realised that he had been guilty of underutilising their experience and knowledge for so many years. Part of it was the Canberra culture, the notion that ministerial and policy advisors were somehow superior to the electorate staff. But most MPs and Ministers knew that having a fabulous ministerial office was no good if you didn't have an electorate, so the electorate offices were crucial to keeping them in Parliament.

A wealth of ideas came out of the lunch and by the time they had finished their meal, topped it off with lattes all round, they had a plan that would involve policy forums. Rob would publish papers on their findings and the implications for policy. He had come to realise that there were several people in the office who would be well able to draft the papers themselves, and resolved to get them involved.

The enthusiasm was such that by the time he got back from his next trip to Canberra the first forum was totally organised. It was to discuss education, as this was one of the issues that they received the most complaint letters about. Letters had been sent out first to those who had made related complaints or had registered an interest in the area. The first was held in his office, and attracted twenty-five people, which wasn't a bad start. They had decided to break the proceedings into two parts. The first would be to identify of the issues and problems and the second would be to propose possible solutions. The decision had been to make these forums as informal as possible so that people would not feel too intimidated to have their say and, if the amount of talking was any indication, people felt very relaxed! His constituents were surprised and flattered that their MP was interested in their ideas for improving the education system, and they weren't going to miss the opportunity to have their say.

Rob and his staff started writing up reports on their findings and distributing them to his colleagues on the feedback they were receiving. Over the next twelve months they held a further ten forums. Rob was stunned at the response they got and the willingness of people to tell them how they felt. Some people were so pleased that they volunteered to help set these events up.

Rob finally felt like he was getting somewhere; moreover, that he was getting back to the things that had prompted him to go into politics in the first place. He felt as if he was shifting back to his previous beliefs and suddenly he was unsure about some of his current attitudes.

However, a challenge was going to come from closer to home which would really make him rethink his position on a lot of things.

Jack had started at university and was loving it. Suddenly the Connors' quiet and reserved son had found his voice, and was extolling his views – ad nauseum. Rob was reminded of himself at university and was pleased that Jack had come into his own. He and Maggie had been a little surprised, as neither of their children had shown any interest whatsoever in politics prior to this. Neither foresaw the problems that would be caused by this in their family.

Jack began to express his newly found political views over dinner, and very interesting political discussions ensued, given that three family members had a strong interest in the area. Samantha often finished her dinner quickly and went upstairs with a disgusted look on her face, obviously finding her homework more interesting.

At first, Jack just seemed to be flexing his muscles and trying his ideas out. His opinions indicated a very left stance, and for that Rob was grateful.

At night in bed Maggie and Rob often discussed their son's rapid development into manhood. They were very supportive of him and pleased that he was doing so well.

One night over dinner Jack said in his quiet, assured way, 'Dad, how could you have justified being part of a Government that introduced HECs and the Austudy supplement?'

Rob drew in a deep breath, surprised at what his son had said. Then, convinced that Jack would understand, he attempted to explain his Government's position. 'We had a crisis Jack, we needed to find a way to fund more university places, and students are not being asked to pay money back until they are earning a reasonable wage.'

Jack looked his father square in the eye and said, 'I'm sorry, Dad, but that is complete bollocks! You must have done the sums. These students are going to leave university with huge debts. You know as well as I do that you have simply opened the door for the Liberals to up the HECs and make sure that university is not an option for anybody who isn't rich. They will simply put the repayment threshold amount down so that students will have to make repayments, despite earning a small wage. It's a disincentive to going to uni at all.'

It was hard to tell at this point who looked more shell-shocked, Rob or Maggie. Rob recovered himself first and said, 'Jack, we never would have put up the HECs rate; the Libs did that. You need to be angry with them for using the policy irresponsibly, not the Labor Government.'

Jack stood and stared at his father. 'Dad, seriously, how can you look me in the face and use that argument? You introduced the policy – you can't take the moral high ground on this because they increased the rate. It was your Government's idea.'

It was hard to tell who was more upset at this stage, and Jack announced that he was off to bed. Maggie and Rob watched him walk away. Rob was hurt, and shook his head as if to rid himself of the memory of the discussion. He had taken a lot of criticism about his policies – but from his son! Maggie made them a cup of tea and they retreated to the verandah.

'Wow,' she said, 'I don't know whether I'm impressed, shocked or hurt. Which one of us is responsible for the straight-talking, no-pulled-punches style?'

'I'm not sure,' he mumbled. 'I don't suppose I can look for any support from you on my moral high ground position?'

Despite herself, Maggie laughed. 'Oh, I don't really know. Largely I have been proud of your position, but I am a different person now from the one who worked in Canberra, and I would have to rethink my position on a lot of policies nowadays.'

Rob's head shot up. 'Are you serious? You might not agree with your earlier positions? But you thought them through thoroughly when you supported them, didn't you?'

'Yes, of course I did – you know I did,' she said. 'But I am really different now. I am not sure that he is wrong, and it's not just because I worked for the other side. Of course, I disagree that people like my father are simply trying to keep everyone but the rich out of universities.'

'What bit do you think is right then?' Rob mumbled petulantly.

'Well, Mr Sulky,' she said, laughing, 'did you really think that the Libs wouldn't put up the HECs, or put down the wage at which students would have to start repaying?'

'We thought it was a possibility,' he said, 'but we can't be responsible for what the Libs do.'

'No,' she said, 'but you didn't think at anytime that you were making it possible for the Libs to make students' lives harder? Didn't you think that you were making such a move relatively easy for the Libs? Once you had set up the HECs scheme, it was always going to be easy for them to make it more severe, wasn't it?'

'Well, we thought about it a bit, but you don't understand we were confronted with a real problem in funding universities,' he replied.

'Of course I understand that, you nut! I worked there as well, you know,' she said.

'I know, I know,' he grumbled.

'The point is,' she persisted, 'is that Jack obviously thinks that you must have had other options. He clearly feels that you guys sold students out. Remember, before you went to Canberra, you were idealistic as well. You would not automatically have agreed to a solution like that when you first arrived. You had to be indoctrinated into believing that there were very few options open to you so that you wouldn't dare try to introduce anything radical and pro-students. Jack is still filled with the courage of inexperience and still believes that it is possible to make genuinely good policy. Frankly, now I agree with him. It seems sad to me that to survive in Canberra people need experience and a thick skin, yet these are actually the qualities that ensure we are no longer capable of introducing really sound policy and changing the world, the way we had wanted to when we first went there!' She stopped to take a deep breath, having surprised herself with her outburst.

Rob was overwhelmed. He knew his son didn't understand politics and government, and the difficulties making and implementing policy – but his *wife*!

She had been there, she knew. How could she think that?

They went to bed that night with a lot on their minds. For the next few days Rob spent a lot of time thinking the conversation through and came to no significant conclusions.

Although Rob was hurt, Jack seemed fundamentally unfazed by it. In fact, not a week later he started another contentious discussion, this time on the treatment of asylum seekers.

'Oh man!' Samantha grumbled and left the table again.

'Dad why doesn't the Labor Party have a more humanitarian policy on asylum seekers?' Jack asked.

'We have a more humanitarian view on asylum seekers than the current Government,' Rob answered.

'Well, that's not saying much!' Jack responded indignantly.

'You need to understand that most of the voters are of the opinion that they want a hard line on asylum seekers, to crack down on those abusing the system and potential terrorists. If we hadn't recognised the views of the voters, then we had no chance of getting into Government and therefore no opportunity to change policy,' Rob answered.

'So your party thought that it was okay to send the message to voters that you would be hard on asylum seekers and refugees in order to get elected? You would abandon them and risk sending families, children even, back to death and torture – all to get into Government?' Jack argued.

Rob took a breath and made the mistake of speaking to Jack like a child in an effort to avoid a serious disagreement. 'Well, you know, Jack I think that you need to understand the realities of Government. If you are not in Government then you can't change anything, and sometimes you have to reflect what the electorate wants to get in.'

Jack flushed. 'And what, Dad, makes you think that you deserve to be elected if you aren't prepared to have the courage of your convictions? Have you forgotten that Government is supposed to lead – not follow on like sheep? Surely if the electorate believe something you don't agree with you should educate them and show them why you believe that they are wrong... give them an opportunity to change their views.' He pushed his chair back, and announced that he was going to bed.

Rob sighed heavily and looked over at Maggie.

'Checkmate,' she said with an eyebrow lifted, and got up to get her husband a cuppa.

'He is so disappointed in me,' he said when Maggie brought his tea out.

'Don't be so silly, love,' she replied. 'He loves you and he is proud of you, he just doesn't always agree with you. You and I used to disagree with each other all of the time on politics but we still loved and respected each other.'

He had to concede that she was right, but Rob still went to bed with a heavy heart. His son couldn't know that he had hit him in his soft underbelly. Rob had never been comfortable with his Party's recent position on refugees. He had felt that the Government had been trading on the fear that people had felt after 11 September and had exploited this to take a hard line on refugees. Rob's party had chosen not to take an opposite line on this as they felt that it would compromise their bid for Government. Yet many had felt uncomfortable about it.

He remembered the Pham family, who had been his neighbours when he was younger. Bao and his sister, An, were a lot younger than him, and Bao had once told him the story of how they came to be in Australia. Bao told him how they had sold everything they had to get a place on a boat in an effort to get away from the war which was destroying their country. He told how they had been attacked and robbed by Thai pirates on the way, and his mother and sister, An, had been raped. His mother was then thrown overboard. He and his brothers and father had had to watch helplessly at gunpoint while this happened, and it devastated their family. Bao's father had never gotten over losing his wife and not being able to protect his very young daughter from their attackers.

Rob had felt an ache in his throat the size of his fist and had had to fight hard not to cry in front of this tiny boy who lived next door. He could never believe that this could really happen, it was so far removed from his experience. For years he watched this unfortunate and strong family being treated horrendously by some of the people that lived around them. They had had a snake put in their letter box, and in the very early hours teenagers would throw stones on the tin roof at the back of the house, waking them all up. This was particularly cruel as the Pham family all woke up at 4 a.m. to go to their market garden, including Bao and An. They would come home for breakfast at 7.30 and the kids would go to school and the older boys would go to work. Mr Pham would go back to the market garden and pick all of his children up to go back there at 5 p.m. and they would all work until 10 p.m. They all worked on the market garden six and a half days a week. Bao had told Rob that the reason for this was that their father refused to take any sort of benefits.

Rob woke up in a sweat that night. His addled brain had conjured up the attack of the Thai pirates on Bao's family and he felt ill. He got up and went downstairs for a drink, trying hard not to wake Maggie.

He sat alone on the verandah with his glass of water – a forlorn figure. Was it possible that the roles in his family had been reversed? Did he have to learn from his son on this one?

Soon it was time for the next election. Rob's work, which had so inspired him over the past couple of years, had an additional benefit: he was to win his seat easily. A reward for having invested real time in his electorate.

Jack was to serve him an additional blow during this period. It was the first election that he had been able to vote. Rob had imagined this day and daydreamed about taking his son proudly through the volunteers and their How To Vote cards. Rob had returned to the house for a very quick breakfast and offered to take Maggie and Jack in to vote, so they could vote as a family. Jack took a sip of his coffee, seemingly considering this offer seriously, and then announced, 'I can't vote for you guys, Dad.'

Rob was surprised; he had expected a vote of confidence from his son.

Jack continued, 'I can't because, while I am Labor, you guys aren't any more, so I need to find a left alternative who I consider will actively represent my views in Parliament. You are an excellent local Member but I am afraid that it's not enough. I need someone who represents my views in an outspoken and committed way in Parliament. You will win your seat anyway, and for that I am glad, but I will have protested against the fact that neither major party represents my views.'

Maggie shot a concerned look at her husband. This was a defining moment in her husband and son's relationship. Only she knew the level of stress Rob felt on election days, and she hoped that he would not take this too badly.

Without saying anything Rob got to his feet, and Maggie took a deep breath. He walked over to his son and pulled him to his feet, then he drew his boy towards him and hugged him. 'I am so very proud of you, Jack, and I would be very proud to take you to the polling station for you to cast your first ever vote.'

As they pulled back from each other Maggie noticed

Jack quickly wipe a tear from his eye. She realised that this had been important for him, to have acceptance from his father even when they disagreed on something so important to both of them. She was intensely proud of her husband and son.

Samantha wandered in, bleary-eyed, and, not known for her cognitive abilities before her breakfast, asked, 'What are you guys all up so early for?'

The three of them laughed and walked outside to the car to go and vote.

Chapter Ten

Over the next few months the dinner time politics continued; Rob and Maggie came to the conclusion that they had a responsibility to assist their son to develop in whatever way he chose to go forward. They questioned and challenged him on his beliefs, always trying hard not to allow themselves to take his comments personally. They knew that he was trying to find his way in the same way they had when they were his age. And although they often found the implicit criticism of their own Parties policies difficult, they were so proud of the principled man he was becoming.

Samantha still left the table in disgust when these conversations started, much to the amusement of the rest of the family. She really could not understand their interest in 'boring stuff', as she called it. To compensate for the loss of dinner time as family time, a late breakfast on Saturday mornings on the front verandah had been instituted. Each family member contributed to making breakfast and they sat and chatted about anything and everything, as long as it didn't involve politics. Samantha would often produce her latest wood-related product, and her designs were becoming increasingly good.

Rob, although managing to keep up his end in the discussions on behalf of his party at the dinner table, was starting to seriously review his own positions on policy. He had had the nightmare about Bao and his family on several occasions. In addition he had started to review several of the refugee cases that had come through his office. He had been surprised about the treatment of refugees that he had begun to find acceptable. He wondered when he had found it acceptable that refugees were to be treated in ways Australians would not tolerate for their own people, not even criminals. He had started to feel uneasy about some of his current policy positions, wondering whether he had really moved so far from what he had believed when he had first become involved in politics. He felt that this time out and the challenges he had experienced at home were telling him something significant, but he also felt that the ground beneath his feet was shifting as well. What if the outcome was that he began to disagree with his Party's position? He had seen this happen before and he knew that some Party members were not that forgiving of members who betrayed the tribal Party loyalty.

He needed someone to speak to whose opinion he could trust and who would not pull their punches. Then it struck him. Who would have a unique view of what he had believed in his early years of political involvement? The answer was clear – Johnno, his first boss. Johnno was an old leftie from way back and had often made comments about Rob selling out the Party, in what Rob had always taken as jokes. He had certainly never been having a go, but what if he really thought that Rob had sold out? He hesitated for a week or so before finally finding the courage to make the call.

'Well, hello, my old love,' Johnno bellowed on the other end of the phone line, 'slumming it, are we?'

After getting his hearing back, Rob laughed, he had forgotten how much he missed Johnno's sense of humour.

'Feel like lunch?' he asked his old boss.

Johnno agreed that lunch would be an excellent idea.

'None of the old places,' Rob said, meaning Sorrento's or Botticelli's. In several of the eateries around town, they could not avoid seeing colleagues, and this was not the sort of conversation he wanted to have to worry about people overhearing.

Johnno had always been a clever bloke and he knew a potential life crisis when he saw it. He suggested a tiny place in Subiaco, blessed with tiny nooks and crannies, ostensibly designed for students who needed a quiet place to study. They made arrangements for the following day and rang off.

The next day Rob had a quake of nerves as he got in the car to meet Johnno, but he managed to pull himself up and get on with it. He couldn't leave things as they were; he needed to sort his thoughts and beliefs out once and for all.

Johnno was already there and well into his first latte by the time Rob arrived. For a working-class boy, Johnno was a coffee connoisseur, and rarely passed up any opportunity to indulge his passion. He rose when

Rob joined him and gave him a bear-like hug.

They sat and ordered lunch with a smashing Spanish red. Rob had decided on a steak and kidney pie – a bit of comfort food – and Johnno decided on the fillet steak with a Béarnaise sauce. Finally they were left alone to chat, Rob had no idea how he could bring up the subject that he felt he needed to discuss with Johnno.

Johnno asked him how Maggie was and was very impressed to hear that she was working on her third book, and that Jamie was expecting it to be a hit as her first two had been.

'Damn, that girl can do anything she puts her mind to,' declared Johnno, clearly impressed by Rob's wife, 'not bad for a Lib! And how are those delightful progeny of yours?'

Rob laughed, 'You have no idea. Samantha is creating wonderful wooden things and has decided that she wants to be a cabinetmaker.'

Johnno raised his eyebrows, clearly impressed, but he didn't interrupt as he had a sense that they were close to the subject that Rob wanted to discuss.

Rob continued, 'Jack... well, Jack is the biggest surprise of all. He is at university studying to be a teacher, he has also become an established leftie. Who knew that my quiet boy would become a poster boy for the left?'

Johnno knew that somehow they had hit on whatever it was that was bothering Rob so he stayed quiet and waited.

Rob sighed heavily, not knowing quite where to go from here. Their food arrived providing him with a temporary reprieve. For a brief moment he considered not bringing the subject up at all.

For a few minutes they ate their food in silence. Finally Johnno decided enough was enough, he needed to help Rob out here.

'So what's on your mind, Robbo?' he asked. 'You look like you have the weight of the world on your shoulders.'

Rob sighed again. 'I just don't know where to start.'

'From the very beginning, my boy, from the very beginning,' his mentor stated.

'I have started to rethink what my positions are on things,' he said, guilt rendering his voice to barely a whisper.

'What sort of things?' Johnno asked.

'My position on policies,' Rob answered. 'I have been accused of selling my soul, and for just a moment I wondered if they were right.'

'Oh!' was Johnno's response. 'And have you?'

Rob's face flushed, 'I guess I'm here because I think there is at least a chance that I might have.'

'And what does Jack have to do with all of this?' Johnno asked, showing, yet again, some of that amazing insight that had so surprised Rob in his early years.

'Ah,' Rob replied, and his companion saw real pain in his face. 'He is the one who's pointed out the error of my ways. He thinks I have sold out my principles and,' he paused swallowing, 'he didn't even vote for me.'

Johnno was really hurt for his protégé but he was impressed by Jack. Most people hadn't had the courage to tell Rob that they felt he had moved away from the values and ideals that had brought him into politics in the first place. It wasn't just Rob; most politicians who went on to bigger and better things were forced to give in to pragmatism, or at least felt they were. It was hard not to feel disappointed when you supported a talented, ethical MP, only to find that once they had the power to actually change things, they fell short of expectations. It wasn't as simple as that, of course. They came under intense pressure from those groups who had supported them and felt the stress of governing for the whole country – including those who didn't vote for them or agree with their policies. Soon they found themselves finding compromises to keep everyone happy. In fact, such compromises rarely kept anyone happy.

'And do you think he is right, Rob?' Johnno asked softly.

'I don't know, I really don't know,' Rob answered. 'Maybe he is right? His views aren't fully developed yet but some of his comments have hit me hard. He had a go at me about asylum seekers and I have been having nightmares. There is just a chance that he is right on that one. God! Have I really sold my soul?'

Johnno knew this was serious; he knew what it had cost Rob to come and talk so openly to him about this.

'Rob, there is only one person who can answer your question. If you are asking me whether I think you were different when you worked with me, then the answer is undoubtedly yes. You were young and idealistic and full of ideas to fix the ills of the world. But let's be serious here. You couldn't maintain that level of idealism when you became a Minister. It is a hard job and there are a lot of people to please.'

Rob looked up, grateful, but Johnno continued, 'Rob, I have always admired you and I think you must be one of the most clever and capable people I know, but if I am truly honest with you I have been disappointed with some of the policy decisions you have made and chosen to support. I feel that you have squandered opportunities to really change things in favour of appealing to the majority.'

Rob sobered up, he was hurt and yet somehow strangely grateful that this man was prepared to tell him the truth. Somehow he really knew that the uncomfortable feeling growing in his gut was real. He wasn't just having a midlife crisis, he knew that he had to rethink his position across the board. And surprisingly, he had his son to thank. Despite the hard road ahead and the amount of aggravation he was going to cause his former colleagues by altering his position – they would simply see him as a troublemaker – it was a move he had to make.

The point was that he had to be true to himself and stand up for what he believed in. God, it was so simple, and yet it would be so hard to actually do! Suddenly he sat up straighter in his chair, and from his changed body language Johnno felt that a decision had been made. From the look on his face he felt relief that this man had found his way through something that had the potential to bring him down.

'Well?' he asked.

'Johnno, I don't quite know how I am going to sort this out, but I do know that I am about to become a thorn in the backside of the Parliamentary Labor Party,' Rob replied.

Johnno roared with laughter and bellowed, 'I'll drink to that!'

The two continued their discussion late into the afternoon and Rob left exhausted but happy. He had a huge job in front of him in trying to get his head together and working out the way forward on all of this.

Over the next six months Rob met with many community groups whose task it was to represent refugees and asylum seekers. He was surprised anew at how clever and committed these people were in their work to protect the rights of refugees. What surprised him more were the allegations of mistreatment of those in detention centres. He felt sure that such mistreatment was in no way the Government's intention but equally he knew that they could be doing more to protect these people.

There had to be place where competing interests could sit happily together. Rob was passionate about this issue. He knew, despite how uncomfortable it was about to be, he had to step outside his own Party's policy. Alternatively, he thought optimistically, maybe he could help rewrite it.

He put together a group of informed people who would confidentially provide him with advice. Within a few short months he had what he considered to be a very clear picture of the refugee situation in Australia. In Rob's opinion, given Australia's standard of living, Australia took on a comparatively small number of refugees.

Rob knew that ordinary Australians would never want legitimate refugees sent back to places where they were at risk of torture or even death. Although his countrymen were not exposed to such tragedies of the human condition, most were good people who were supportive of the underdog. They would not subscribe to a policy that would be responsible for innocent people's deaths. Therefore, the issue was to demonstrate to voters that without a robust process to ascertain whether incomers were legitimate refugees or not, death really could be the result. Such a policy would need to address Australians' fear of terrorists entering the country under the guise of being asylum seekers. Rob had never seen any evidence of this occurring, but it was important to reassure people that it could not occur, that the system would protect them.

There was a good system of tribunals and courts in place to determine whether a person was a legitimate refugee, but in recent years the Government had cut back funding and, in Rob's opinion, access to the adjudicating bodies. He felt that the key to a successful refugee policy was a robust process where people and their representatives were able to state their cases in front of objective, independent, fair and well-informed people.

Rob, his staff and those in his small committee began to draw up policy drafts in relation to Australia's handling of refugees and proposals to better fund the justice systems relating to their cases. These papers were distributed to his Parliamentary colleagues for comment.

Rob was very pleased with the processes that he and his team had gone through to develop what they considered was a firm and, more importantly, fair approach to asylum seekers. He was totally unprepared for the response he received.

First his office began to receive support from several very relieved MPs who had been uncomfortable with what they had perceived to be an unfair approach to people coming from truly awful circumstances. But that wasn't all the feedback they received.

Unexpectedly, one of Rob's very senior colleagues 'visited' him in the office. After the expected enquiries about family and a superficial discussion about their fellow MPs and high profile issues, the visitor, Jeff Kramer, got to the point of his call. Rob had been wondering if his colleagues were wanting him to consider coming back to the frontbench in advance of the next election. He was aware that the Government had made some headway in their claims that the Opposition was without an experienced frontbench, since their leader had made way only months before for a younger, less disciplined version – Andrew

Matheson. The implication was that the Opposition could not form an effective Government if elected.

Jeff took a deep breath, and the second before he spoke Rob's optimism began to waver. He did seem to be taking this discussion rather seriously.

'Rob, there has been some discontent about your recent approach to policy on refugees. I am sure that you can see how inappropriate it would be for us to appear soft on refugees this close to an election. The public want a tough stance, and frankly we are going to have to give it to them if we want to win the next election,' Jeff stated in a matter-of-fact manner.

Rob was totally floored. Far from being offered a position on the frontbench, he was having his knuckles well and truly rapped.

'So what exactly are you saying, Jeff?' he asked.

'Oh, I wouldn't want this conversation been two old friends to get uncomfortable. But we will not be in a position to change anything if we are not in Government.'

Oh my God, Rob thought, he is using my own old arguments against me! He said, 'Jeff, this Party has always prided itself on having open and robust discussion and debates on policy. This discussion is happening within the Party, and frankly I think that it is an important one to have. This is not about presenting a soft image on refugees to the public, it's about examining all options and better meeting the needs of all concerned.'

'Yes, yes,' Jeff replied, clearly dismissing Rob's point

of view. Then he adopted a softer tone. 'Rob, we all want you back on the frontbench, but as you know it is critical – particularly having just chosen a new leader – that we present an entirely united front.'

Rob managed to contain his dismay. Surely Jeff couldn't have meant that if he didn't retreat on this issue his chance of coming back to the frontbench was at risk? Was he being told to keep his mouth shut? He managed to keep the remaining minutes of their meeting congenial and retreated to his office after he saw Jeff out.

His shock soon subsided and was replaced with anger. How dare they try this on! Still, he had to think deeply about it all before moving forward.

He decided to give himself an early mark and go home. He needed to talk it through with someone, but not until he had had a chance to go over the issues by himself. He got most of the way home and decided to call in at the Subiaco restaurant Johnno had taken him to only a couple of months before. He wasn't sure whether he wanted to run into Johnno or not but he did need a quiet place to think. He found his way there and was just about to seat himself when he heard a familiar voice. To his surprise warm relief flooded over him in response, and he poked his head around the corner.

'Rob, my old love,' Johnno boomed. 'Here for a spot of late lunch, then?'

Rob nodded in agreement. By some miracle Johnno had been planning to eat alone and had a bit of time to spare before he had to be back in Parliament.

'Well, I don't like to be so blunt, but frankly you look bloody awful!' Johnno remarked.

Rob laughed. The day that Johnno didn't mean to be blunt he would be six feet under. He hesitated for a minute, knowing that telling this story to Johnno would be regarded as a serious lack of loyalty if it ever got out. Then his anger rose again and he decided to throw caution to the wind.

'I had an impromptu visit from Jeff this morning,' Rob stated flatly.

'Jeff Kramer?' Johnno asked, unable to keep the distaste out of his voice.

'Yep – he came and gave me the "for us or against us" speech,' Rob said. Johnno waited silently while Rob continued. 'He has basically told me that any possibility of me returning to the frontbench depends on my loyalty to the Party… in other words, retreat!'

'So what are you going to do?' Johnno asked.

'That's what I came here to work out,' Rob replied. 'Y'know, I'm so bloody angry! Years of work, and all for nothing. I can be stopped from taking my place back on the frontbench because I dared to raise some issues that frankly I think are important enough to discuss. Years of work and effort for this Party seem to count for nothing.'

'That's a bum rap,' Johnno said thoughtfully. 'D'you remember Damion Jones?'

Rob groaned, 'Come on, Johnno, that was totally different! We were in the middle of an election campaign, and he comes out with a public statement that we were selling out the environment! Plus, I didn't threaten him with his job, I simply pointed out that there might be a better time to have this discussion than two weeks before the election.'

'Well, as matter of fact, as I understand it, his job was threatened by those who shall remain nameless. Although whether any of them were in a position to deliver on this threat is another question, Damion clearly thought they were. He also said that he had repeatedly tried to raise these issues during his first term and had been ignored. He decided that the only way to get the profile he felt it deserved was to raise it then,' Johnno stated flatly.

'Well, if that happened I can assure you I knew nothing about it, and I would have put a stop to it had I known. Frankly, I think our record on the environment is reasonable – not great, but reasonable. The issues in that election were so clearly health and employment, and we were desperate to get our message out on those two issues. The polls were coming back that the public was angry about the Government's treatment in these key areas, and we were not succeeding in communicating our policies. Then along comes Jones, and all of sudden all of our work goes down the toilet and we are back to square one! The papers and TV media were full of Jones's claim that we sucked on the environment. We were set back two whole weeks, and you and I both know that is time you never get back in an election campaign. *And*,' Rob continued, really irate now, 'who the hell did he think that he was? He was twenty-seven years old and had been in Parliament for five minutes – and thought his opinion was so important that he could throw an entire fucking election!'

Johnno grinned, 'Fair enough... So, given all that, why do you think you should be treated any differently?'

'Because I have earned my stripes and I happen to think we are wrong! I have not gone public on my views; I have followed a time-honoured tradition of developing policy within this Party. We are not in the middle of an election, we are more than a year away. I am clearly not trying to destabilise Matheson, even though what the hell he is doing running this Party is totally beyond me!' Rob exploded.

'So what made you think that taking a stand on this wasn't going to cost you? Geez, Rob, for a smart man you can be dense. If it was easy to change the views of this Party it would be happening all of the time. People want to change it and make it as good as it can possibly be, but they get stopped in their tracks for a variety of reasons, most of which are simply about the time and very hard work required to do it. Many quite rightly believe they are entitled to a life as well as a job. What you are proposing is hard work, and it will cost you. You don't get to be the hero of refugees without it costing you. So don't give me any bullshit, Rob, just think about this: what price are you prepared to pay? Some problems don't need rhetoric, they need action – and this is one of them.' Johnno's voice was harder than usual.

'God, you think I am trying to do this to be a hero?' gasped Rob, horrified at Johnno's harsh words.

'Rob,' Johnno spoke more gently now, 'I have rarely met anyone with the potential that you have. But truly you have coasted for most of your political career. For the first time I see you looking like you are prepared to step up to the plate, and you have come to me for advice. I can't fail you here. This is really important, you really are in a position to make things happen. This is not the time for me to piss in your pocket.' Johnno coughed and went on. 'Rob, I would have been so proud of you if you had become Prime Minister, and you would have been a good PM – a damn sight better than what we have now, that's for sure. But what I see before me is the beginnings of a man who could be a truly great Prime Minister, perhaps one of the best this country has ever seen. You have two choices here, Rob, and only you can decide what road to take and how much you are prepared to sacrifice for it. But I am not going to be your apologist, and what's more I think you knew that when you came here today, and that is why you came.'

Rob was speechless. If he'd come here confused he would go away more so. He hadn't thought this was about his leadership aspirations. Maybe Jack was right. Maybe he had to earn his right to be Prime Minister, and not just with the Party. Maybe a lot of people thought being better was not enough.

Chapter Eleven

The next few weeks were really tough for Rob, he had taken a beating from two of the people he cared most about and Maggie, although understanding, hadn't been as supportive as he would have thought she would be. For heaven's sake she had been there, she knew what a cut-throat world politics could be. There just wasn't a bloody thing you could do if you were not in Government and, despite what everybody said, the voters of Australia could be a conservative lot. Jack could get all high and mighty about it, but it was no small feat trying re-educate people on political issues in a nation where the sports pages were the most read part of any newspaper. Not that he blamed them, he was prone to reading the sport's pages first himself. Rob appreciated that he had spawned an idealistic and interested son as opposed to the alternative, but it was easy for people to throw their comments in from the cheap seats. Look at Johnno, a terrific Member of Parliament, his constituents loved him and with good reason, his everyday (well, every weekday anyway) was about making life better for them. But he wasn't an ambitious politician and probably with good reason, he didn't have to be all things to all people – manage a massive department, fight for its rights and funding alongside the good of the Party, the good of the

Government and the good of his constituency. He was very clear about his priorities and life had dealt him a hand where he would never have to choose between such massive competing priorities.

Rob felt bad for thinking like this, but fuck it all – he was meant to be Prime Minister. He had known it all his life, he was clever, capable and competent. There were bugger all Prime Ministers who could boast all three of the necessary C's. He really had it – charm, intellect, no bloody awful skeletons hanging out in his closets. The media had tried and failed to make an issue out of Maggie's father and her previous work for the Liberal Party.

He had busted his arse for years for his constituency, for the Party and for various departments and what did he have to show for it? Now he was getting kicked in the teeth by people who had no bloody idea what it was like, how hard it was and how bloody thankless it was. He knew he was being ungrateful, especially to Johnno who had given him his first chance in politics, and who had supported him over so many years – acting as his mentor. Some bloody mentor to kick him in the teeth right when he needed support most.

It was over a bottle of red one night that the growing bile spilled over into something a little less pretty. He was no longer able to escape that uncomfortable feeling in the pit of his stomach. He knew that down very deep, in that place that no one knew about, that no one could see, he needed to be Prime Minister, he needed it like he needed air to breathe. It wasn't just about wanting to be Prime Minister, he craved it with a hunger that frightened him. His everyday was filled with the fear of not achieving that ultimate external approval – he needed Australia in all of her wonderful, terrible, fantastic, breathtaking entirety and he needed her to need him.

Even with everything he had been blessed with in his life he had been unable to quell the hunger inside. Standing down as Leader after that devastating defeat and finding himself as backbencher had made him stare into the abyss that was absolute, immutable failure. His mind and willpower had drawn him back from that place and now he was convinced that it was not over for him, the fear had been replaced again by the desperation to take his place as the rightful overseer of his great country. He could not allow himself to see any other possibility, he could not bring himself to that precipice again, because he was not sure that, if he did, he would be able to bring himself back from it.

He knew he should want it just for what he could do for his country – what was that old JFK saying, 'It's not what your country can do for you, but what you can do for your country'. He knew it at some level and he had no problem presenting to the world the Rob Connor that wanted to serve his country. Because, at some level, it was true and because of the significant runs he had on the board, people pretty much bought it. He had never had an issue 'proving' his credentials for running as Leader of his Party. Let's face it, he was the right man for the job, all this toing and froing over inadequate leaders since he had stepped down had proven that. Maybe he had been wrong to insist on stepping down; he had never really believed it would be long term; in some unacknowledged place it suited him that they hadn't had a successful leader since him; he wanted them to need him back.

It was during these dark days, with growing anger and bitterness at the fact that he wasn't in his rightful place and at those around him feeling free to kick him while he was down, that he had an almighty row with his wife. It was a very rare occurrence, they often had little arguments, but had never really had enough time to engage in all out warfare. He had been moping about the house, annoyed and annoying and had driven her completely mad. Maggie had spent much of her time in politics stressed and aggressive and had come to realize that this was not the person she wanted to be; she had striven to create a harmonious environment in their home, making it a haven for her family from the stresses and tumbles of the world. Rob's mood pervaded every corner of the house, everybody was affected by it and she began notice that for the first time in their lives the kids were choosing to be somewhere other than at home, sensing a mood they were uncomfortable with. Perhaps more worryingly she had noticed that her normally very moderate drinking husband was partaking of their merlot at a greater rate than she had previously seen. She had tried on countless occasions to discuss it with him, but he simply refused to be drawn on what was on his mind. Finally in an unguarded and unprecedented response to his aggravating behaviour she snapped, 'Rob what the hell is wrong with you? You are like a bear with a sore head, everyone is sick to death of you. Spit it out or get over it.'

Rob was furious – couldn't she see that he was having a hard time? Talk about being unappreciated. Of all people – she should understand what was going on with him. He glared at her, unable to find the words to explain how he was feeling.

Maggie mistook the silence for obstinacy and spat, 'I really have had enough Rob, you are making life in this house impossible. You are not the only one who lives here you know!'

He was completely floored, how could she say that to him? How could she be so insensitive as to be missing what was going on with him? She knew how hard he had worked. She knew the people he worked with and how much better he was than them. Suddenly it all began to spill out, words tripping over each other in an effort to be heard. He raged about the state of the Party, how hopeless the leaders were and how he was being silenced by people who didn't know what they were talking about and couldn't care less about the policies produced by the Party anyway. He ranted about how no one understood that if they weren't in Government they couldn't change anything and how everybody was a bloody armchair expert, telling him how he had failed, when he was the only one who was really out there trying to make things happen for the people on the street. They needed to win and he needed to lead them for the sake of the people, the people shouldn't be left to the whims of Gooring and his crew. He even went as far as to suggest that the only person who could bring this country back to what it was supposed to be was him, they needed him before it was too late.

Maggie had gone silent, her face was like a mask, her feelings unable to be read from her features. Then in an eerily quiet voice she said, 'The most important thing in politics is sincerity, once you can fake that Robert Connor you have it made.' Then she turned and walked out of the room her heart pounding with a strength of feeling she had never known. On her husband's face she had seen for the first time a shadow of the moral deadness that is at the heart of many politicians. In his rage against the unfairness of the world she had seen what he had tried so hard to cover, to keep to himself, that the first and foremost concern in his life was about winning – about being Prime Minister – not about the good of the country but about being given the ultimate seal of approval. She shivered knowing that there was only one cure for this deadly disease and that was total and utter failure. How could she wish that cure on the man she loved more than any other in her whole life? She was disgusted and sympathetic all at the same time. She had seen this take over the lives of lesser men and she could no longer pretend that he hadn't been afflicted as well. She could only hope that he could find some sort of real balance between the interests of himself and his country, because he was right – his country needed that. She also knew that at some level he was also right about himself, she had been around politicians all her life and he was simply the best option available at the present time. She knew despite this devastatingly uncomfortable confirmation of one of her deepest fears, that he was a good man with a network of people who would be able to help him maintain a healthy grasp on reality if he ever got the opportunity to be PM again.

Rob stood stock still in the lounge room, his shoulders stooped, suddenly looking like an old man. She had seen it! She had known what was deep in his soul. He knew she was right, he knew at some level they were all right, but he knew with a dreadful certainty that the possibility of success was still there, however, remote and as long as it was every fibre of his being would strive for it. He was suddenly afraid that having seen this side of her husband she would reject him and he knew that he would find it impossible to do this without her love.

He walked through to the bedroom where she was sitting silently on the edge of the bed. He sat next to her, she pulled his head to her chest and they sat like that for a very long time.

After a tough weekend pulling himself together, Rob walked back into the office full of determination. Although better understanding his motivations and not being entirely comfortable with them, he knew that the end was the same. He had decided that at some level Johnno was right: he had coasted along thus far. If he was going to fight for his right to be who he was and who he wanted to be then he had to prove that he was worth it, that what he stood for was worth it. If he turned away as soon as the going got really tough what would that say about him?

He called his team together for a lunch meeting and they determined their next step. They would contact all of the MPs and other Party members who indicated their support and invite them to a forum to discuss the issues around refugee policy.

Two weeks later, sixty-five people had made their way to the community hall in Wilson. His small team had done an impressive job organising the forum and several people had agreed to speak on the issue to kick off the discussions.

Within fifteen minutes, they were well into a healthy debate and by 4 p.m. that afternoon they had agreed to a strategy where all involved had committed to conducting an internal Party campaign to get MPs and Ministers onside to encourage more debate and hopefully a change in policy. There was a sense of optimism and Rob's team had agreed to coordinate the campaign. Fact sheets and case studies were developed and Rob felt that he and his team could not have developed a more constructive way forward.

The next few weeks were event free, life progressed smoothly and all of the information they had gathered was distributed as expected. Rob felt sure that even Jeff Kramer would have to consider that this had been a constructive approach to this issue.

Life at home was going well, the harmonious equilibrium having returned. Maggie and he had found their way back from their conflict with a greater, if less pretty, understanding of each other. And who was to say, maybe it was better if you could find your way through times like this with no illusions. It was never referred to again, but Rob felt it was not far from the surface for either of them. It was a sort of knowing that could never been undone or reversed.

Jack was doing really well at uni and thoroughly enjoying it. Maggie was totally convinced that he had a girlfriend but all her guarded inquiries had revealed no information thus far. Debates were raging at home as to whether Samantha would complete year twelve or go straight from year eleven to Tafe. Maggie was insistent that Samantha complete year twelve as she felt that this would give Samantha a better base for her future should she ever change her mind about what she wanted to do with her life. Samantha was insistent that she would not change her mind and while Rob suspected that she was right, he also recalled that in her short life Samantha had wanted to be a jillaroo, child care worker, travel agent and a horse trainer. This cabinetmaker idea had lasted much longer than the others but Rob had to concede that Maggie was right, an investment of one more year at high school was sensible just on the off chance that she changed her mind down the track. But to Samantha an extra year was 'for ever'. Finally Rob and Maggie resorted to a bit of bribery. Samantha had wanted a scooter to get to and from school for some time. They had bought a Mini for Jack to get to and from uni when he was accepted into teaching. Therefore they offered Samantha a scooter if she successfully completed year twelve and got into Tafe to do cabinet making. They felt a bit cheap but felt that on this occasion the end justified the means. Samantha accepted the offer and they knew that she would put in the minimum effort but fortunately, in Samantha's case, that would be more than enough to get a reasonable Tertiary Entrance score.

Maggie had decided to take a break before completing her fourth book and was happily renovating the kitchen, which hadn't been done in some time. Jamie had called to say that a production company was interested in turning her books into a TV series and Maggie was characteristically unsure of herself. Jamie, on the other hand, in his overwhelmingly confident manner, was sure that this was exactly what Maggie should be doing. Maggie had decided to take a few weeks out to decide. She had been looking tired lately, but Rob thought that if he had to keep builders and electricians to plan all day everyday he just might look tired too. However, he filed away that he may need to plan a holiday, even a weekend away, to return the rosy glow to her cheeks. Some sleep and good food should fix the dark rings under her eyes.

Politically, Matheson was leading Gooring in the polls and, aside from the fact that he was a loose cannon, often made his policies on the run and had a habit of being undisciplined, he seemed to be keeping the show on the road.

Overall Rob was very happy with the world; however, he was to receive a phone call that would pull the rug out from under his feet.

He had arrived at the office fairly early and gone to make himself a cup of coffee. No one else had arrived yet and he often enjoyed those first few quiet moments in the mornings. It wasn't to last long, two of his staff burst through the door just as the phone started to ring. They got to it before him and then his phone buzzed and he was asked whether he would take a call from Jerry Hicks, political commentator on one of the more sensationalist tabloids.

Hicks, he thought, I haven't heard from Hicks since I was the Leader of the Opposition. Why would he want to speak with me now?

He took the call.

'Hey Rob howarya?' Jerry asked, 'So what do you have to say about this refugee stuff?'

This refugee stuff? Rob thought, what could he be referring to? Surely he can't be referring to the internal campaign.

'What refugee stuff are you referring to Jerry?' Rob asked, keeping it light, but he did have a knot growing in his gut.

'Don't play dumb with me Robbie. The stuff you've been doing that's pissed Kramer off.'

Rob's mind was racing, how the hell could Jerry know about that meeting?

'Jerry I have to go now, I have another call waiting,' Rob said replacing the handset. He knew Jerry would be really annoyed at being fobbed off but he had to find out what was going on before he spoke to the press and Jerry was not the most trustworthy journalist at the best of times.

He was just contemplating who to ring to find out what was happening when his old pal Steve called. He hadn't heard from him for months so was a little surprised by his call. After the requisite questions about family, Steve came to the point, 'I don't know what you are up to down there Rob, but you sure have set the cat amongst the pigeons up at HQ. Kramer's got his knives and his boys out.'

'What's he done Steve?' Rob asked, the knot growing larger by the minute.

'Well, one of his boys has leaked to the press that you are trying to destabilise the party and it is sour grapes on account of the new leader being so much younger than you. They are setting you up to look like a troublemaker who has lost the plot,' Steve said gravely.

God this was about as bad as it gets. The press were like vultures, they would smell a carcass and the heat would be on Rob until another, more sensational story came along.

'Damn this is really bad, what the hell am I going to do Steve?' Rob asked anxiously, 'Which media has picked it up?'

'Only the trash thus far,' Steve replied, 'the clever media won't pick it up until they have done some checking and, given the way the troglodytes are representing themselves, they may not pick it up at all.'

But Rob knew that Steve was only trying to make him feel better.

'Do you want to tell me about it?' Steve asked quietly.

Rob gave Steve a run down of the events and Steve gave a low whistle, then laughed. 'Well, good on you, Rob, this has certainly scared them that's for sure. Hope you are ready for this though because it could get even nastier,' he said, getting serious again.

By the time they ended their phone call they had organised to meet late the next day and Steve would ensure that Gary O'Brien was available on the phone. They would work out a strategy for dealing with the press interest. In the meantime Rob was to keep busy and keep the press at arms length, if they got to him he was to laugh off suggestions that he had lost the plot and take the moral high ground at suggestions that he would do anything to destabilise the party he had worked for most of his life.

Rob was a touch shaken but knew his survival in politics was crucial and depended on his capacity to deal with issues such as this. It was ridiculous that their limited time and resources was to be spent responding to such malicious gossip. However, he wasn't the first and he certainly wouldn't be the last to be in this position. Sad but true. His thoughts turned to Steve and Gary and how lucky he was to have them to help out when he needed them even though they no longer worked with him. He hadn't even needed to ask – the help was offered.

His computer beeped to inform him that he had an email. He clicked on the tiny envelope. A little wary at first he roared with laughter. The email was from Johnno and read, 'Don't let the bastards get you down!'

He realised that this information would filter down to his staff if it hadn't already. For this reason, and the fact that he had always believed that he should keep his staff informed and involved so that they all felt part of the work they were doing and the decision making, Rob decided to call an impromptu team meeting.

From the expectant looks on the faces of a couple of his staff, he had his answer. They were certainly aware that something very significant was up. As it was nearly lunchtime he asked that one of them organise some lunch to be brought in and suggested a team meeting. He said he had something to discuss with them and noted their mixed looks of surprise and pleasure at the thought that he wanted to discuss what was on his mind with them. As he walked back to his office, he thought, not for the first time, how much unnecessary secrecy there was in politics.

Lunchtime came more quickly than he thought and they popped the answering machine on. After a brief hesitation he updated them on the events of the past day. Surprisingly his staff had made the connection between Jeff Kramer's visit and the events of the past few hours. He advised that Jeff had suggested that the timing wasn't good to be raising contentious issues such as refugees' rights when the Party had just selected a new leader. One staff member raised her eyebrows without a comment. Another asked whether he was planning to drop the campaign, there was silence as he answered, indicating that he needed to seriously consider what happened from now and consult on it, but no, he thought that it was most unlikely that he would drop the campaign. He asked them what they thought the team should do about the refugee rights campaign and they unanimously agreed that they would like him to continue, even if it meant they were all on the outer with the Party for a short while. He was impressed as hell by their commitment.

Together they developed a strategy for the next day and a half before Rob could meet with Steve and speak to Gary. Before he walked away he thanked them for their support and hard work and as he returned to his office he was overwhelmed by how many people had chosen to cover his back at a very difficult time. This decision could cost each of them and yet they had all chosen to do it instinctively, as if they had expected their commitment to the cause to cost them personally and professionally. Yet again he reminded himself of how much he had to learn from his team.

Aside from a plethora of calls both at home and at work the next thirty-six hours went reasonably smoothly. He left at 2.30 to meet Steve closer to his city office and when he arrived he was stunned to see Gary O'Brien sitting there as well. For a brief moment Rob felt emotional and wasn't quite sure what to say,

Gary had clearly flown all the way from the Eastern States to help him out. He fought the lump in his throat for a moment before Gary stated in his characteristically sardonic manner, 'Well, you just don't like being out of the news do you?'

Rob was grateful as the brief threat to his self-control had passed. The three sat down over a cup of coffee and tore the problem apart. By the end of the meeting they had decided that Rob would give an exclusive interview to the 7.30 Report who not had engaged in any speculation. He would tell it as it was. Make it clear that he never had been, neither would he be a destabilising influence in the Party. He believed in democracy and for that reason he would support the new leader, and he referred anyone who would like to question it to his record. He would take the opportunity to highlight that there was an internal discussion happening inside the Party to determine whether the Government was protecting all interests in the refugee debate and that this in turn highlighted the fundamental difference between the two major parties: Labor was prepared to debate and discuss their policies to ensure that they came up with the best policy alternatives, the Libs were not. Rob was very happy with this approach.

Two nights later he was to find himself on the 7.30 Report and he delivered the approach to plan. The interviewer was someone he was comfortable with, firm but fair. A phone call from Steve at the end of the interview confirmed the outcome – checkmate.

When he got home, feeling very proud of himself, he found that Maggie was in bed. Samantha said that she hadn't been feeling well. She lowered her voice as she said, 'Actually, Dad, she has said that a few times in the last few weeks, do you think she has a virus or something?'

Rob stopped to kiss the top of his daughter's head and replied, 'I'm sure it's nothing sweetheart but I'll check okay.'

He was disturbed by the look of relief that flooded his daughter's face, bounding up the stairs he found Maggie lying in a restless sleep. Her face was very pale and she seemed to have sweat on her forehead despite the chilly weather. He sat down beside her and stroked her hair for a few minutes. Then he walked outside on the balcony, a feeling of dread came over him and he knew in that minute that he should have been taking more notice of things at home.

The next morning he rang in and let them know that he had an appointment and that he would work from home when it was finished. The team were buoyant about the interview and he rang off feeling happier.

He took a cup of coffee to Maggie in bed. She sat up, her face pale and the rings under her eyes very apparent now. She smiled at him, 'To what do I owe this pleasure Mr Connor?'

'It's been far too long since we had brekkie together,' he said.

'Oh God,' she gasped, 'I am so sorry – how did your

interview go? I can't believe I forgot.'

'It was great, just as Steve and Gary predicted,' he replied.

'What's wrong?' she asked suddenly suspicious.

The phone rang and Samantha yelled up to say that the builders wouldn't be coming because of the rain and that she was off to school now. They both yelled back telling her to have a good day. Rob was relieved that they would have the day to themselves.

But Maggie wasn't going to let him off the hook so quickly, 'What is wrong Rob?'

He considered trying to bluff her but then decided that he may as well tackle this one head on.

'Maggie I am really worried about you. You look tired and you are not sleeping well. Sam says that you have been complaining about not feeling well.'

She quickly looked away but not before he could see the dismay in her eyes. She turned back to him, 'It's nothing Rob. I am just having a few tests.'

Rob was horrified why hadn't she told him about this.

'Tests, what tests? And why didn't you tell me about this Maggie?' he asked.

She sighed, looking unhappy and very, very tired, 'I have been feeling really run down lately and I went off to see Derek, he suggested some tests. They are due back this afternoon. There was no point telling you about it, there really isn't anything to tell.'

Rob was shell-shocked, 'What is he testing you for?'

'A range of things,' she replied, 'He doesn't really

know what to look for yet.'

'I am going with you this afternoon,' Rob stated.

They debated the topic for a few minutes but Maggie could see that his mind was made up and frankly was relieved. The rest of the day passed slowly with Rob making them both breakfast and then suggesting that she have a rest before the Doctor's appointment.

They got in to see Derek just after 2 p.m. and he looked a touch bemused, which did not cause them to relax.

'Maggie, I don't quite know how to say this but you are pregnant,' addressing them in that direct way that doctors often do.

They both laughed. 'It's not possible Derek,' Maggie said, 'I am on the Pill and, well, I am old.'

'Sorry Maggie, I have run the tests three times, you are having a baby. I know you are on the Pill, but you must have had an upset stomach or something, that can often cause the pill to be less reliable. Some vitamins can even reduce the effectiveness of some contraceptive pills,' Derek answered.

Rob and Maggie looked at each other in shock, Samantha was seventeen this year, they hardly expected to be having another baby at this stage in their life. They left the surgery with instructions for Maggie to come back and see Derek once she had had a chance to absorb the news. Derek had congratulated them on the way out, but such was the shock that it barely registered.

When they got home Maggie said that she really needed to lie down and have a rest and then they would talk about their little surprise. Rob took Maggie upstairs and tucked her in. They talked momentarily about how amazing it was that they could have made another little life at this stage in theirs. Shock had well and truly been taken over by wonder.

An hour later Rob heard Maggie call him, he walked up the stairs and found her on the floor. He rushed to lift her up and saw pain etched in her face, she was gasping for breath.

'Rob take me to hospital now, something is very wrong,' she breathed. 'Help me please.'

Rob started to panic, Maggie was the tough one in these circumstances, what could he do?

He grasped her arms and half carried her down the stairs, bundling her into the car. She moaned with agony and her face broke out in a sweat. He drove out onto the road like a maniac and then took a deep breath. Maggie was counting on him to get her there safely and he had to pull himself together.

The drive to the hospital was traumatic. Maggie was crying in pain, grasping her stomach. Her face was dripping with sweat and she kept muttering that she was going to pass out.

Rob couldn't bear it, his beloved Maggie in so much pain and he couldn't do anything to stop it.

It seemed to take hours to get to the hospital emergency entrance. He parked the car in a emergency bay and yelled loudly to some waiting ambulance officers, 'Help me, please help me.'

Somehow there was a stretcher and Maggie was

loaded carefully on it. The officers, seeing the amount of pain she was in, pulled her into the emergency waiting area quickly. The place was packed with sick and injured people, Rob began to panic again realising that Maggie may not be seen for some time. Maggie was to resolve that problem, she screamed in agony and promptly passed out. Suddenly a doctor and several nurses appeared and the stretcher was propelled behind some swinging doors and into a very primitive cubicle. Within seconds they had established that she was pregnant and Rob was pushed, unwillingly, out of the cubicle to a waiting nurse to provide details. The doctor came out from behind the cubicle curtain to advise Rob that Maggie was at best miscarrying and at worst she had an ectopic pregnancy. He advised Rob that he suspected the latter and for that reason he wanted immediate permission to get her into surgery as there may be risk of a rupture. Rob nodded his consent and was allowed in to see Maggie for a very short time as they prepared her for surgery.

'My love it's going to be all right, you are going to be all right. And I will be right outside waiting for you. I love you Maggie,' he said, holding her hand as they wheeled her out of the cubicle.

The nurse advised him that he could use the phone. Rob was momentarily confused as to why she had told him this and then realised he had to let the kids know, and her parents! He rang his mother not having any idea what to do next. She told him not to worry, she would let everyone know and she would be there with him very soon. He hung up the phone and shook for a few moments, before being interrupted by a tap on the shoulder. It was one of the nurses with a cup of tea, she led him into one of the sparsely furnished relatives' rooms. Suddenly he was totally alone. He felt desolate, in all of the other crises in his adult life Maggie had been with him. Now the person he would have turned to was critically ill, he was totally alone and could do nothing to help her. The tears ran unchecked down his face. Suddenly he found himself praying, 'God, God I know I don't deserve to ask you this but please, please don't take my Maggie away. Please, please help her get better.'

His gut wrenched and he felt fear in every pore of his body. He was sweating pure fear, he could smell it on himself. He knew he had to pull himself together, Maggie would need him. His kids would be here soon and they would need him. He took a swig of the ghastly tea and felt the sugar kick in, control started to slowly seep back into him.

The door opened beside him, Derek stood there looking very sombre, 'They called me, I am so sorry Rob. There was no sign of this when you came in this morning. There often isn't you know.'

'She will be okay, won't she, Derek?' Rob asked, desperation evident in his voice.

'I hope so Rob but if it is ectopic and it has ruptured it can be very, very bad. I know that is not what you want to hear, but I won't lie to you,' Derek answered.

Rob put his head in his hands and the tears started again. Suddenly he heard Jack's voice, 'Where is he?

Where is my father?'

Rob sat up and wiped his face quickly with his hands. He had to protect and help his children now, they really needed him.

Derek stood up and waited until the room filled with people, he nodded to Rob as he left.

Samantha ran over to her father, 'Daddy, Daddy is Mum all right?'

He hugged her and pulled Jack into his arms as well. Then he indicated that they should all sit down, his parents and Maggie's were there as well. He wondered at how quickly his mother had been able to get them all there. Ingrid and Geoff looked dreadful, shock evident in their faces.

Rob explained the day's events from when they had found out about the pregnancy through to everything he knew now, which he realised suddenly was not a great deal. As soon as he finished the questions started, the kids were stunned that their mother was pregnant, but no more so than his and Maggie's parents.

There was a tap at the door and Derek beckoned Rob outside.

'It's bad Rob, really bad. There was a rupture and they are operating right now but she has lost an enormous amount of blood. They are going to have to give her a blood transfusion,' he said gravely.

This hit Rob like a ton of bricks, he swayed and Derek reached out a hand to steady him, 'Are you saying that I might lose her? Tell me you aren't saying that she might die.'

'I can't Rob, they are doing everything they can but there is a chance that they might lose her, she has lost a lot of blood. They did say the fact that you got her here so quickly was very helpful,' he added.

There was a rushing sound in Rob's ears and he fell forward. Derek, in a rare show of sensitivity, propelled him out of sight of his children. He slid to the floor and leant against the grey tiled wall.

Derek knelt down beside him and forced his head between his bent knees, telling him to take deep breaths. The moment passed and Rob recovered his breath. His mother, having realised that something was very wrong, had left the room and come to kneel next to him. She held his head in her arms while he sobbed great, gasping silent sobs.

As he stood up Geoff and Ingrid came to join them. Derek helpfully explained what had happened. Geoff seemed to collapse from inside and Ingrid turned and held him firmly in her arms until he was able to stand by himself. Tears fell silently down her face and she said, 'We need to go back now and tell those children that there is no way in this world that their mother would leave them. Are we ready?'

The small group walked slowly back to the relatives' room to comfort the children. Geoff had recovered and he told the children in a strong, if halting voice, what had happened. Jack and Samantha fell into their father's arms and he held them tight as he told them that their mother was the strongest person he knew and that there was no way she was going anywhere.

They sat silently in the room for some time, forcing down cups of undrinkable tea. It seemed to be hours later that the tired doctor came to the door. He looked exhausted and very solemn. Fear clenched Rob's gut again as he turned to listen to him.

'Mrs Connor has come through the operation. She has required an enormous amount of blood and the next twenty-four hours will be critical. However, I have rarely seen a patient rally so strongly as this one so I feel optimistic that she has a good chance of pulling through,' he nodded to them before turning away.

'Doctor, can we see her?' Rob almost shouted.

He turned back, 'Yes, but one at a time and only for a couple of minutes. She is not conscious yet though. Nurse will you take Mr Connor through to his wife?'

Rob leapt from his chair and followed the nurse, willing her to walk faster. She opened the door to a small room and there was his beloved Maggie. Her face was chalky white and there were tubes everywhere but he could see the rise and fall of her chest so he knew that she was alive. He walked to her side and picked up her hand, it seemed small and cold. He held it to his cheek as if to will the energy from his body into hers. Gently and carefully he leant across her body to place a kiss on her pale lips.

'I love you Maggie,' he said. 'Stay with me, my love, I can't do it without you.'

He sat beside her and stroked her hand for a few minutes and then all too quickly the nurse was back at the door with Jack. He left the room, giving his son a comforting squeeze on the shoulder as he walked to the door. He stood outside waiting for Jack and soon it was Samantha's turn. Jack joined his father outside, pale and clearly unsure of himself. Within a very short time Samantha had joined them and they left the area free for her parents and then his own.

When everyone had seen her, his mother decided to take Jack and Samantha back home and to stay with them so that Rob could stay the night at the hospital. Geoff and Ingrid decided to stay as well and they decided to take turns sitting beside her bed.

Several hours later, Rob was sitting on one of the hard, uncomfortable chairs in the relatives room and had dozed off into an exhausted sleep. He woke as someone was shaking his shoulder, as he opened his eyes he heard Ingrid say, 'She's awake Rob, she's woken up.'

Rob leapt from his chair and sprinted to the small room. A nurse put a hand on his arm and indicated that the doctor was in the room and that he should wait a moment.

Five minutes later the doctor walked out and said, 'She is a remarkable woman your wife. She is doing very well and although she is not entirely out of danger the signs are now very, very good.' He gave Rob a tired smile and then walked away.

Rob walked quickly into the room and Maggie looked up and saw him come in. She held her arms weakly out to him and he took her hands. They looked at each for a long moment, then he moved forward taking her in his arms gently and held her while she sobbed. Great racking sobs came from her weakened body and he thought that his heart would break to hear her. Finally she stopped and he sat down next to her. Crying seemed to have taken all the strength she had and very soon she slipped back into a fitful sleep. He walked out to tell her parents how she was doing. As he walked out of the room, he saw Ingrid fall into her husband's arms and he realised that she felt she could fall apart now that she knew her daughter would be all right.

Later that day, the doctor confirmed that Maggie was officially out of danger.

A week and a half later, Maggie was allowed to go home under strict instructions to rest. Derek had promised to stop by every couple of days to check on her. It was not until she was safely in bed and tucked in that Rob went downstairs and thought about what had just happened. He had nearly lost the love of his life without any warning at all. He felt a changed man, life was too short to spend on anything that wasn't really important. So what was important to him? His family and standing up for what he believed in. He needed to spend more time with his family; he had not even noticed that Maggie was sick. The time he spent away from them had to be worth it. He did not have time for pettiness and small 'p' politics anymore; he'd rather be at home.

It was an uncompromising Rob Connor that met with Jeff Kramer two weeks later. Kramer was extra nice, asking after Maggie and thinking that Rob wouldn't feel that this 'little refugee thing' was important now with everything else going on in his life. The entire office heard Rob state very clearly and concisely that he did think that the 'little refugee thing' was very important. He was no longer going to play silly buggers with Kramer and his cronies, if they didn't like it they could lump it. He was going to push this and any other issue that he considered was crucial. He had entered Parliament to change things and he had wasted enough time, now was the time for action.

Kramer was obviously stunned, he blustered about Rob losing his chance at the frontbench and his own need to 'protect the Party'.

Rob simply answered, 'You do what you must do Jeff and I will do what I must do.'

His team watched open mouthed as Jeff Kramer stalked out of their office and then turned to Rob.

'Well, I suppose that we had better get on with it now that we have said that we will,' he laughed and turned back to his office.

Three months down the track the Labor Party was forced to concede that it needed to rethink its policies on refugees.

Chapter Twelve

The months after Maggie's return home went slowly. Rob worked from home a lot, and his parents and Maggie's visited often to help out. There was one upside, Maggie finally agreed to a cleaner helping out a couple of times a week. The house had been Maggie's domain since they got married and she had never agreed to having someone else clean it for her. Jake was a fabulous cleaner and even cooked a couple of meals. His cuisine was a touch exotic for Jack and Samantha's taste, but at least Maggie was convinced that they weren't being neglected.

Maggie had spent two weeks in bed looking completely shattered. She was very emotional and entirely drained. She knew that she was unlikely to ever be able to have another child and, even though they had never planned to have another baby, the fact that she now couldn't seemed to have affected her greatly.

Derek dutifully visited every two days for the first couple of weeks until he was sure that Maggie was healing well and being well looked after.

Ingrid, Geoff and Rob's parents visited often and brought dinners when they came. Geoff and Ingrid had had a terrible shock that genuinely seemed to have aged them and they spent a great deal of time with Maggie.

Jamie and Paul visited a lot, often staying for barbecues with the family once Maggie was back on her feet. They brought the food and drinks and provided plenty of entertainment.

Rob was overwhelmed by the support and care that was around to help Maggie and her family. All of his family and friends were extra sensitive to Maggie's need for rest and to their family's need for time by themselves.

Rob spent quite a few nights after Maggie's return just wondering if she was going to be okay. Afraid to go to sleep in case something happened to her, he would sit in the old cushioned chair in the corner of their room and gaze at her while she slept. She was so incredibly precious to him. How did he ever lose sight of how important she was to him? He hadn't thought that he had lost sight of it. He had just become more and more involved in his work and in his desire to become Prime Minister he had momentarily lost touch with what was really important. He had to work out a way that he could spend more time with his family.

Jack and Samantha, who had spent every available waking moment with their mother after her return, had now settled back into their own routines.

One afternoon when he returned from a short meeting at the office Rob walked in to find Maggie lying on the couch reading a book. She looked up as he came in and smiled at him. He saw that the colour had returned to her face and he realised that she had turned the corner both physically and emotionally.

'So, honey, how did your meeting go?' she asked, sitting up to greet him with a kiss.

Rob gave her the bare bones of what had been a fairly unremarkable meeting.

'I have some gossip,' she announced.

Rob raised his eyebrow in question, 'What sort of gossip?'

'Gossip that will cost ya!' she said, grinning.

'Will a cup of coffee with a chocolate biscuit do the trick?' he asked, returning the grin. His Maggie was definitely back.

'Yup,' she said, settling herself back on the enormous couch.

Two minutes later, having delivered his side of the bargain, Maggie began, 'Jack has a girlfriend.'

Rob sat up straighter in his chair, 'No way – how do you know this?'

Maggie laughed, 'I have been watching him and I accidentally overheard him on the phone. Haven't you noticed the distracted look on his face lately?'

Rob had, he had thought it was to do with the fact that he had nearly lost his mother, but he wasn't going to bring that up now.

Maggie whispered, as though concerned that the kids would hear her, 'I think her name is Hannah.'

'How do you know that?' Rob demanded.

'Well, I answered the phone the other day and it was a Hannah for Jack, and when he took the phone he blushed. I am sure that I didn't imagine it.' Maggie grinned wickedly.

Rob was terribly impressed by this piece of detective work and said, 'I wonder how long this has been going on?'

They would not find out the answer to that question for some time. However, they were to meet the elusive Hannah.

Rob had decided that he was going to take his family away for a short break. He was very keen for Jack and Samantha to come along and felt that the likelihood of this happening would increase if they were allowed to take friends with them. He raised the idea with Maggie, she was keen and very much wanted the kids to be there too. One night at dinner Rob raised the possibility of the holiday with Jack and Sam. Both were surprisingly keen to go, and were happy to bring friends along.

It took some time but, as they tucked into banana ice cream, Jack announced that he would like to bring his friend, Hannah. Maggie nearly choked on her dessert and then asked sweetly, 'Who is Hannah, darling?'

Jack mumbled something about Hannah being his girlfriend and, true to form, Samantha ran with the idea and teased him mercilessly for a good ten minutes. Rob eventually suggested nicely to Samantha that unless she wanted equivalent treatment when she had a boyfriend, she should quit now. While this didn't halt the flow for long, it was enough for Maggie and Rob to learn that Jack had, unsurprisingly, met Hannah at university. She was doing law and wanted to be a legal aid lawyer. They couldn't fail to be impressed by this choice; it already told them significant amounts about the girl who had captured their son's heart.

Within a few days the holiday was pretty much planned and the following week they were off. Rob had rented an eight-seater van, and after a quick breakfast they all bundled in to head off to Madora Bay. Samantha had decided to bring her friend, Trudy, a quiet and reserved girl, a remarkable contrast to their own daughter. The much-anticipated Hannah was a total surprise. She was a lively, good-natured girl who filled in many of the quiet moments left by Jack. Maggie and Rob were amazed to see how fascinated Jack was with his inamorata. He would gaze at her for long moments. He made no attempt to cover his feelings for Hannah, and vice versa. Hannah was a very demonstrative girl and they were surprised to see how Jack took to her: holding hands and constantly kissing. Sitting across from them in the small café they had stopped in for lunch Rob looked across to Maggie and their eyes met. Suddenly he knew that she was having the same sense of fate he was: Hannah was part of their family for the long haul. He had always known that it would happen like this for Jack; he had never been frivolous with his feelings.

Samantha was a joy on the holiday and Trudy was a faithful and easy companion. Rob and Maggie watched both their children – well, not really children anymore – as they exploded onto the beach outside their holiday cottage. Samantha and Trudy were exploring everything and looking for the best spots to keep an eye on boys. That was proving no difficulty, given the number of surfers visible from their own small part of the beach. Hannah and Jack had found a secluded spot and were sitting holding hands and chatting... well, Hannah was chatting and Jack was gazing.

The sun was setting as Rob and Maggie sat down on the wooden chairs on the verandah. The sky flooded with purple, orange and pink, and for a brief moment Rob decided that his life could not be more perfect. He looked across at his wife who was staring wordlessly out at the horizon, taking it all in. Her face was lit by the mesmerising glow of the sunset. He noticed the small lines around her mouth and eyes and thought that he had never seen a more beautiful woman in his whole life. He had never really understood what middle-aged men saw in younger women. Nearly all of the women he knew, and in particular his wife, had grown more beautiful and infinitely more sexy with age. He was very attracted by the independence and assurance that came with age. Maggie turned to him and smiled, he felt his heart flip over in the same way it had done when he first met her so many years before.

The holiday was much better than they could have hoped for. There was a lot of time for family events and yet each of them had time to spend doing their own thing. Samantha had met the love of her life, a seemingly speechless boy more at home 'riding the waves' than spending time with Samantha's family.

Samantha was enamoured with him from their first meeting and although Josh seemed pleasant enough, Rob was at a loss to see what exactly Samantha had fallen for in the tall, gangly, spotty-faced adolescent. Conveniently, Josh had a friend called Sean, who seemed reasonably happy to spend his spare time with Trudy, who was silently approving of the entire thing. She even seemed to chat to Sean, who was a touch more talkative than his counterpart. At night Rob and Maggie would hear giggles for many hours coming from the girls' room.

Rob and Maggie each had a lot of time to speak to Hannah, and were unsurprised to find that despite her vivacious personality she was deadly serious when it came to her career and political beliefs. Rob attempted to avoid all discussion on his Party's political position as he felt quite sure that Hannah's outlook would be very similar to Jack's. However, Hannah was most happy to keep the subject on philosophical opinion rather than specific policy areas, with the exception of justice-related issues. As a lawyer himself, Rob found himself in complete agreement with Hannah's assessment of the legal system in Australia, and admired her commitment to trade off money earning potential to go and work for legal aid. In a funny sort of way that is what he felt he had done, sacrificing money to work for what he believed in. As a lawyer Rob could have earned so much more, although he was aware that most of the Australian public would not agree that he had sacrificed money for his beliefs. It reminded him again of the challenges that he had faced recently and would no doubt continue to face over the next few months. Again, he reminded himself that surrendering his earning potential was only worthwhile if he stood up for what he believed in.

All too soon they had to return to real life. It was a wrench for all of them; the barbecues on the beach, the relaxation time they'd enjoyed, sun and sea had done them all good and they were loathe to get back to work and study. Samantha was less than pleased about leaving her beloved Josh, and there were many promises of emails when she returned. It seemed to Rob that Josh was just as disappointed to see Samantha leave as she was to go. Trudy was a touch more stoical about her separation from Sean, although both appeared pleased at the prospect of being able to report a summer dalliance – not that they said so in so many words.

A relaxed and suntanned Rob found himself at work the following week. His staff allowed him time to get himself a cup of coffee before dumping the past fortnight's work on his desk with what appeared to be barely suppressed glee.

After a few hours solid hours trudging through the never-ending paperwork on his desk, Rob was interrupted by a phone call from Steve.

After a few minutes talking about Rob's holiday Steve came right to the point. 'Rob, I hear on the grapevine that Gooring is in serious trouble.'

Rob straightened in his chair. 'What's going on?'

'He has been caught out in a few untruths lately but I gather there is a storm cloud brewing that has the potential to take him out. I hear that he is planning to call a snap election to decrease the chances of it getting out before the election.'

Rob let out a low whistle. 'What could be bad enough to take him out?'

'It seems that there is some suggestion, as yet unconfirmed, that he has been putting pressure on Department officials to blur the edges in reports for some time now and the word is that it has finally crossed the line, and Department heads are getting bolshie about it. There is some question that there may have been a deliberate omission about some intelligence recently that may have had a direct impact on our involvement in the Iraq war. Word is that someone might actually be prepared to blow the whistle,' Steve replied in his quiet, self-assured way.

Rob let that information sit for a moment, just long enough for Steve to continue. 'Rob, that's not all. As we all expected, Matheson is not coping. Some of his past stupidity is coming back to burn him. The journos are treading lightly because most of them hate Gooring as much as we do, but they can't hold out for ever. He is a loose cannon, and now he's a loose cannon that may end up Prime Minister.'

'Sadly we can't do anything about that, Steve, we just have to hope that he can hold it together until after the election,' Rob replied, very thoughtful now and somewhat frustrated that his Party had not put a better man in the job in the first place. It would be fatal electorally to have a leadership challenge at this point if the election was as close as Steve thought it would be; but now they were facing being in Government with someone who was incapable of running the country. To make things worse, that someone didn't realise he wasn't up to the job.

Steve rang off and they made plans to catch up the following week over a drink. Rob found it difficult to dismiss the conversation from his mind, and even more difficult when he realised that there really wasn't anything he could do about it at all.

To his great surprise Jeff Kramer 'dropped in' again for a chat the following week, ostensibly to see how he was faring. After a reasonably polite conversation about their families Kramer got to the point, 'I certainly hope that recent unpleasantness about the Party's asylum policies is no longer a sticking point between us, Rob. Anyway, now the Party has changed its view on this issue, we can move on.' He smiled jovially in attempt to carry his message further, the smile not making it anywhere near his eyes. Rob was bemused, but managed to be equally polite until Kramer finally took his leave.

After Kramer left Rob realised that the reason for his visit had been to ensure that Rob did not work against Matheson in the forthcoming election. On the one hand Rob was amused that Kramer felt that he had that much power, and on the other he was annoyed that because he had fought the Party on a policy area, they thought he would deliberately try and sabotage the Party's election chances.

That night he got home to a buzzing house. They had a full complement for dinner, with Hannah and Trudy over. Maggie had the whole team actively involved in preparing for the impromptu barbecue. He was home only minutes before he was given his orders by General Maggie to go upstairs, change his clothes and then stoke up the Weber. He was downstairs in minutes, aware that to stand in the way of the progress was to earn many black marks with his wife. The Weber was duly stoked and Hannah and himself were sent outside with the meat and marinated chicken to cook it. Hannah turned out to be a star, within minutes she had him entirely organised. Rob watched her, impressed at her 'just do it' attitude. He realised all of a sudden that in many ways she was just like Maggie. No wonder his son had chosen her.

After dinner, while the kids were off doing their own thing, Maggie took Rob upstairs. She showed him her work desk. Sitting on her laptop was the plan for a new book. Book four was in the making and, in that moment, Rob knew that the worst part of the past year was now over.

One week after Rob's early warning, an election was called by a beaming and confident-looking Prime Minister. Rob had to admit that Gooring looked good and wondered how long the smile would last. But not even Rob and his cronies could have predicted the savaging that Gooring was about to receive.

Almost daily, new information came out challenging the Prime Minister and the information and opinions he had provided. Former department officials were coming out and speaking against Gooring and his Ministers. Gooring, though usually stolid, was starting to show the strain. Matheson proved himself, temporarily, to have sound judgment and left the burning at the stake to the media, stating only that he didn't feel it appropriate to comment at this stage, and would not do so until all of the facts were known. It momentarily gave him the look of a statesman, and had the added bonus of denying Gooring the opportunity to play personality politics against him. Gooring could not do so without looking nasty in the face of Matheson's magnanimous refusal to comment on his own ever growing dilemma.

The polls started reflecting the reduction in confidence in the PM, and just when he needed it most Gooring's blind belief in his own ability started to fail him. His face took on a hunted look and his previous polish slipped. In interviews he took a defensive stance and it was clear he had stopped believing that he could win. Ironically, his Party lost any chance of retaining Government because Gooring had called an early election and denied them the opportunity to change leaders. Not for the first time in Australia's history, one man's personal ambitions had cost his Party the election.

The election day came and Gooring was forced to bow – rather ungraciously – out, and Matheson survived his first night as PM.

Rob couldn't help being a touch disappointed that his Party was finally in Government being led by someone who might not be up to the job.

It became inordinately clear that Matheson was suffering from what party hacks called, 'candidate's disease'. He had started to believe that he was, in fact, good enough to be PM. He rejected all suggestions for using experienced ex-Ministers on his frontbench and began to propose stacking it with under forties (significantly under forty, in fact) who had little parliamentary experience, let alone ministerial. His attempts were tempered somewhat by factional negotiations and deals.

Rob laughed as he realised that for the first time in his career he was very happy about the powerful role of the factions in his Party. They were the only reason for some experienced people finding their places on the frontbench when the Matheson Labor Government sat in Parliament for the first time. Rob had been 'canvassed' on the possibility of returning to the frontbench, but he had felt, for a variety of reasons, the timing was not right. He knew after Kramer's visits that Matheson and his cronies did not consider Rob to be onside. He also questioned his capacity to work well under such a leader.

Before long Rob was, sadly, to be proven correct. For a short time Matheson's outspoken views and passion for change was refreshing after Gooring's undisguised conservatism and elitism. There were some uncomfortable moments for Ministers when their leader spoke 'off the cuff' on issues in their portfolio areas. Policy decisions were made in the back of the Prime Ministerial car with young, inexperienced Policy Advisors. On occasion, previously unconsidered policy decisions were made in television or radio interviews. The media were having a field day, often finding themselves in receipt of information on major decisions and having time to 'catch the Minister's office out' before they had been informed. Some Australians loved this new PM, who simply made decisions on the spot and did not seem to be hampered by all of the things that had stopped previous PMs. The more informed were deeply concerned about 'policy on the run'. Public servants were known to comment on the new Government's 'whatever works' approach. It made those in power look inexperienced and unprofessional. All over the country people were being asked to implement policies that were not thought out and not funded.

Privately Ministers, even those who had been somewhat enchanted by 'young Matheson' and his cheery good looks, were expressing doubts.

Unfortunately things were to take a turn for the worse about six months into Matheson's reign. In an ABC radio interview, when confronted by a rather conservative woman from rural NSW, Matheson announced that his Government was going to punish parents for not making their children go to school. It took some hours and the efforts of a persistent reporter before the Minister for Education became aware of this new 'policy'. Understandably, he was completely horrified. Not only was this approach on the right wing end of Government, but education was largely an issue for State Governments and this remark was bound to cause huge consternation.

When they returned to Parliament the following week the Liberals were hugely amused by the situation the new Government found itself in on its latest education 'policy'. The State Governments were furious and traditional Labor supporters and interest groups were up in arms about the fairness of such a policy. Privately, the new Liberal Leader, Malcolm Cherry, told Rob that there was no way that the Liberals would have ever considered such a policy. In fact, he doubted even that One Nation would ever consider such a draconian approach.

Rob was concerned for other reasons. He had seen such a policy operate in the United Kingdom, and a mother had even been sent to jail because her children refused to attend school. She had claimed, quite accurately, that aside from using physical force, she could not 'make them' go to school.

Rob could not imagine how any Government could justify such an approach, when Tony Blair had raised it he had wondered whether he was in a parallel universe. How had Blair managed to ignore his own responsibility for the safety of children at school? Rob felt sure that, like Australia, many schools had considerable problems with bullying, violence and drugs. In addition there were significant numbers of high school students in Australia who were leaving school illiterate and innumerate, he felt sure that this was true of the UK as well. No wonder children didn't want to go to school if they did not feel safe or felt as though they were not learning anything! Rob had always felt that the answer lay in dealing with the reasons children did not want to go to school and he could not see any value in sending their parents to jail.

Criticism was coming from all angles on this one and, fortunately for all, the Minister, an old hand, had recommended that a review take place on the value of such a policy. The Minister was able to spin this approach as a sign of the new Government wanting to ensure that its policies were best for people rather than simply running ahead and implementing them; it wasn't a back down by the new PM, which would have been political suicide at such an early stage in his reign.

It was at this stage that many in the responsible media were starting to get twitchy. They had supported Matheson because they had wanted rid of Gooring, whom they had felt had a negative impact on Australia; however, they considered the new guy a complete flake. This resulted in the shortest honeymoon period for virtually any PM in Australia's history, and the knives came out in a totally unrelenting fashion.

Matheson's personal and professional history was out there for the whole country to see. While he knew that no politician was perfect, Rob was stunned that Matheson thought he could get away with running for PM with some of the 'mistakes' he had made. The old saying in politics is that the Liberal Party is always in trouble for sex and the Labor Party is always in trouble for money. Matheson seemed to have managed to straddle both parties in this respect. He was in trouble for both and – from what Rob could see – lots of it! There was a steady stream of people from Matheson's past prepared to come out and do the dirty on their old pal, the Prime Minister.

Rob and his staff watched the drama unfold day after day. It was so appalling that it had an air of fiction about it. Rob wondered how he could ever have thought that Andrew Matheson was inexperienced. He certainly had experience in some things, if all of the stories in the media were to be believed!

It was therefore no surprise that two months after the onslaught had begun, a mere eight months into Matheson's Prime Ministerial term, Jeff Kramer made another visit to Rob's office. Rob knew that the views of all of the more senior Labor Party MPs would have to be taken onboard concerning who would replace Matheson. What was a surprise is that by the time Kramer slunk into Rob's office on that Tuesday morning, it was not for an opinion on contenders to replace Matheson, it was to tell Rob that his colleagues had unanimously identified him as the next PM of the country...

Rob knew he should play it cool. His dream was now in his hands. He excused himself to ring Steve who, being the best informed person in the WA State Government, was sitting by the phone waiting for his call.

'What the hell do I do, Steve?' Rob asked. 'How do I play this? I guess I need to make them work for it now.' What he had always craved was now within his grasp. This knowledge left him feeling more than a little unnerved.

Steve said gravely and a little harshly, 'Rob, this Party is in serious trouble, and with respect, this is not about you. It's about finding someone who can bring it back together and move it on. Frankly, there's no one else with your experience to become Leader. The Party and the public will see you as a safe pair of hands. This is not going to be the dream job you imagined, it will be a serious recovery operation. *Don't even go there unless you are prepared to do the hard yards.*'

Rob pulled himself back with a start and realised that Steve was right: this really wasn't about him. This Party and the country really did need someone who could pull it together quickly and effectively.

Feeling somewhat abashed, he took himself back to Jeff Kramer, who was looking extremely uncomfortable by this stage.

Rob apologised. 'I am sorry for that, Jeff, I just needed to get my head clear on the implications of this proposal. I need to know from you that I really am the chosen candidate at this stage. We cannot afford any divisions on the decision about who replaces Andrew.'

Kramer brightened up considerably, and provided Rob with precise information. Rob had to concede that the support was overwhelming. This wasn't how he had wanted it to happen, but in a very short time he was going to have to take the reins and be on the ball to handle the difficult times ahead. He knew then that he needed to speak to Maggie.

He turned back to Jeff. 'Jeff, I am sure you know that I cannot walk away from this and see our Party continue to flounder, but before I give you my final decision I must speak to my wife. She is going to need to be behind me 100% if I am going to be able to take this on.'

With graciousness Rob had not expected of him, Jeff Kramer made his exit after making arrangements to speak with him a few hours later. Rob called his staff in and said that he had something to tell them but that he could not do so until he had spoken to Maggie and that he would ring them shortly. From the gleam in their eyes he could tell that they had guessed. He reminded them that it was important that no speculation about what was happening could be made with anyone outside the office because these were very, very difficult times for their Party and conjecture would not help. He knew that it would not be a problem with his staff, who had repeatedly shown their capacity to deal with confidential information.

He drove home experiencing many conflicting emotions. He was excited, but also fearful of the job ahead. He had few worries that Maggie would be against him having the opportunity for him to fulfil his dream, but he also knew the impact that the decision would have on his little family.

He pulled into the driveway just as Maggie was getting out of her car, her arms piled with shopping bags. She looked at him quizzically, clearly surprised to see him home so early. 'Forget something?' she asked.

He smiled at her and helped her carry the shopping inside. Flicking on the kettle in the kitchen, he said, 'Mags, we have to talk, something has come up.'

She turned sharply to look at him. 'Something is wrong.'

Rob smiled again. 'No nothing is wrong, but something has happened and we need to talk about it.'

Coffees made, they went through to sit in the lounge. After settling themselves on the couch Rob told her about Jeff Kramer's visit.

Maggie's face was a picture. She laughed and hugged him hard, then cried at the sheer excitement. Unfortunately it did not take long for her political training to kick in, and she looked at him long and hard. 'Wow! This is going to be seriously tough… You are going to spend at least the first three to six months just making up for the mess Matheson has made. Not quite the way you wanted the dream, is it?'

Rob looked sombre. 'No, it isn't, but Steve kicked me into gear and reminded me that the Party and the country need a safe pair of hands that can pull it together – and apparently my colleagues think that is me.'

'Big job,' Maggie murmured. Then she grinned again. 'Oh well, you'll give my father and his cronies something to worry about!'

Rob knew that meant that it was okay; Maggie was behind him no matter what and he felt relief flood his body. He really couldn't have even contemplated it without her behind him. They spent another fifteen minutes or so discussing the practicalities of the move to Canberra. Fortunately for Maggie, being an author meant that her job was entirely portable; she could write books anywhere. The kids would require a little more thought, but they were both of an age where many possibilities were open to them.

Rob spent the next few hours ringing Kramer, Steve, Gary and his office. Plans were made hastily and before he knew it the date for the changeover was set. In forty-eight hours Rob was going to take up the reins of the Labor Party. He was going to be Prime Minister. The only condition he had placed on it was that the changeover had to take place in WA amongst his supporters so that he could celebrate with them. The Party machine, keen to ensure that everything went smoothly, was quick to agree.

That night, Rob and Maggie told the kids, and far from being the least bit worried about the practicalities, they were delighted for him. Hannah had come to dinner as well and she was equally pleased. When they began to discuss living arrangements, Rob noted that Hannah and Jack exchanged a furtive look. Rob and Maggie waited for the inevitable announcement.

'Dad, Mum – Hannah and I want to move in together. We have been thinking about it for ages,' Jack stated, waiting apprehensively for his parents' response.

Maggie looked at Rob and he nodded. She replied, 'Jack and Hannah, we are very pleased for you. You are both very sensible, and if you think this is the right time then go for it. In fact, we may be looking for someone to stay here and look after the place when we are not here. It would mean having to have us stay when we are over here, though.'

Jack and Hannah looked delighted, and within minutes they were planning the details of their great adventure. Even the prospect of having his parents stay with them now and then didn't seem to bother them.

A small voice piped up. 'Hey, what about me?' Samantha asked.

Rob replied, 'Well, Samantha, we would love you to come with us, but we also appreciate that you are nearly grown-up now, and we don't want you to have to move to Canberra if that's not what you want. You can stay with your grandparents, I'm sure, or you could come and check Canberra out and see what you think then.' He was grateful for his and Maggie's earlier chat on the subject.

Samantha hastily agreed that she was sure she wouldn't want to leave her friends but there was no harm in checking out the new place. For a brief moment Rob was struck by the thought that his daughter and himself were both to be Cabinet Makers, albeit of very different types.

That night as Rob and Maggie lay in bed Rob began to feel the excitement creep up on him again.

'God, Maggie, I am going to be the Prime Minister in just over a day! I can't believe it – I have wanted it for so long, and now it is finally here I really can't believe it!' Rob said in a loud whisper.

Maggie moved over to pull him into her arms and he could feel her tears on his cheek. 'I am so proud of you, Rob, and you are going to make such a great Prime Minister.'

'But what if I make mistakes?' he asked, suddenly fearful again.

'Rob, the only thing I am sure of is that you will make mistakes, but it's not the mistakes that will determine how you are seen as a Prime Minister, it's how you handle them that everyone will want to see.'

As he finally fell asleep he knew that she was right.

That night he dreamt of the five-year-old in his ridiculously hot clothes announcing to his class that he wanted to be Prime Minister.

Two days later, Andrew Matheson stood up in front of the Parliament and announced that he was stepping down with the following words:

'I need to step down and deal with what the media have written about me. I can't do that effectively here and this country needs a Prime Minister who can concentrate on its needs and not his own. I am very proud to tell you that Rob Connor will be taking my place as the unanimous choice of our Party. He is a well-respected and experienced man who will lead this country in an honourable and honest way. I am sure you will all agree with me that he will make an excellent Prime Minister.'

Rob, who was watching the address on live broadcast in WA, was gratified to see that even the

Opposition had applauded at the announcement that he was taking over.

He had chosen not to speak to the media until after he had spoken with his supporters. The celebration event was to start in half an hour.

Epilogue

He stood, blinded by the camera lights, only faintly aware of the cheering and crying of his supporters. After losing his faith in the sense of fate that had dogged his every day since he was five, he was finally the 'Boss of Australia'. The responsibility of his new job temporarily knocked the breath out of him, tempered only by an overwhelming rush of adrenaline. There was a tiny kernel deep in his soul reminding him that a part of him wanted this just for himself. But perhaps, just knowing that meant that he was less likely to be engulfed by it all.

Taking a deep breath to stop himself becoming overwhelmed by the emotions he was feeling, he put a hand up to still the baying crowd.

'First, I want to say sorry. On behalf of all Australians I want to apologise for the hurt and pain suffered by those indigenous Australians who were denied the right to grow up with their families.'

A deafening cheer rose from the waiting throng and across the land a gaping wound began to heal.